A REALM OF SHADOWS

(KINGS AND SORCERERS—BOOK 5)

MORGAN RICE

D1554482

ISBN: 978-1-63291-442-2

Books by Morgan Rice

KINGS AND SORCERERS
RISE OF THE DRAGONS
RISE OF THE VALIANT
THE WEIGHT OF HONOR
A FORGE OF VALOR
A REALM OF SHADOWS
NIGHT OF THE BOLD

THE SORCERER'S RING
A QUEST OF HEROES
A MARCH OF KINGS
A FATE OF DRAGONS
A CRY OF HONOR
A VOW OF GLORY
A CHARGE OF VALOR
A RITE OF SWORDS
A GRANT OF ARMS
A SKY OF SPELLS
A SEA OF SHIELDS
A REIGN OF STEEL
A LAND OF FIRE
A RULE OF QUEENS
AN OATH OF BROTHERS
A DREAM OF MORTALS

THE SURVIVAL TRILOGY
ARENA ONE (Book #1)
ARENA TWO (Book #2)

the Vampire Journals
turned (book #1)
loved (book #2)
betrayed (book #3)
destined (book #4)
desired (book #5)
betrothed (book #6)
vowed (book #7)
found (book #8)
resurrected (book #9)
craved (book #10)
fated (book #11)

"Life is but a walking shadow, a poor player,
That struts and frets his hour upon the stage,
And then is heard no more."

--William Shakespeare, *Macbeth*

CHAPTER ONE

The captain of the Royal Guard stood atop his watchtower and looked down at the hundreds of Keepers below him, all the young soldiers patrolling the Flames under his watchful eye, and he sighed with resentment. A man worthy of leading battalions, the captain felt it was a daily insult for him to be stationed here, at the farthest ends of Escalon, watching over an unruly group of criminals they liked to call soldiers. These were not soldiers—they were slaves, criminals, boys, old men, the unwanted of society, all enlisted to watch a wall of flames that had not changed in a thousand years. It was really just a glorified jail, and he deserved better. He deserved to be anywhere but here, stationed guarding the royal gates of Andros.

The captain glanced down, barely interested, as another scuffle ensued, the third this day. This one appeared to be between two overgrown boys, fighting over a scrap of meat. A crowd of shouting boys quickly gathered around them, cheering them on. This was all they had to look forward to out here. They were all too bored, standing and watching the Flames day after day, all desperate for bloodlust—and he let them have their fun. If they killed each other, so much the better—that would be two fewer boys for him to watch over.

There came a shout as one of the boys bested the other, plunging a dagger into his heart. The boy went limp as the others cheered his death, then quickly raided his corpse for anything they could find. It was, at least, a mercifully fast death, far better than the slow ones the others would face out here. The victor stepped forward, shoved the others aside, and reached down and grabbed the morsel of bread from the dead man's pocket, stuffing it back into his own.

It was just another day here at the Flames, and the captain burned with indignity. He did not deserve this. He had made one mistake, once disobeying a direct order, and as punishment he had been sent here. It was unfair. What he wouldn't give to be able to go back and change that one moment in his past. Life, he thought, could be too exacting, too absolute, too cruel.

The captain, resigned to his fate, turned and stared back at the Flames. There was something about their ever-present crackle, even after all these years, that he found alluring, hypnotic. It was like staring into the face of God Himself. As he got lost in the glow, it made him wonder about the nature of life. It all felt so meaningless. His role here—all these boys' roles here—felt so meaningless. The Flames had stood for thousands of years and would never die, and as long as they burned, the troll nation could never break through. Marda might as well be across the sea. If it were up to him, he would pick the best of these boys and station them elsewhere in Escalon, along the coasts, where they really needed them, and he would put all the criminals amongst them to death.

The captain lost track of time, as he often did, getting lost in the glow of the Flames, and it wasn't until late in the day that he suddenly squinted, alert. He had seen something, something he could not quite process, and he rubbed his eyes, knowing he must be seeing things. Yet as he watched, slowly he realized he was not seeing things. The world was changing before his eyes.

Slowly, the ever-present crackle, the one he had lived by for every waking moment since he had arrived here, fell silent. The heat that had been pouring off the Flames suddenly vanished, leaving him feeling a chill, a real chill, for the first time since he had been here. And then, as he watched, the column of bright red and orange flames, the one that had burned his eyes, had lit up the day and night incessantly, for the first time, was gone.

It disappeared.

The captain rubbed his eyes again, wondering. Was he dreaming? Before him, as he watched, the Flames were lowering, down to the ground, like a curtain being dropped. And a second later, there was nothing there at all.

Nothing.

The captain's breath stopped, panic and disbelief slowly welling up inside him. He found himself looking out, for the first time, to what lay on the other side: Marda. He had a clear and unobstructed view. It was a land filled with black—black, barren mountains, black craggy rocks, black earth, dead, black trees. It was a land he was never meant to see. A land that no one in Escalon was ever meant to see.

2

There came a stunned silence as the boys below, for the first time, stopped fighting amongst themselves. All of them, frozen in shock, turned and gaped. The wall of flame was gone, and standing there, on the other side, facing them greedily, was an army of trolls, filling the land, filling the horizon.

A nation.

The captain's heart fell. There, just feet away, stood a nation of the most disgusting beasts he had ever seen, overgrown, grotesque, misshapen, all wielding huge halberds, and all patiently awaiting their moment. Millions of them stared back, seemingly equally stunned, as it clearly dawned on them that there was now nothing separating them from Escalon.

The two nations stood there, facing off, looking at each other, the trolls beaming with victory, the humans with panic. After all, there stood merely hundreds of humans here, against a million trolls.

Breaking the silence there arose a shout. It came from the troll side, a shout of triumph, and it was followed by a great thunder, as the trolls charged. They rumbled through like a herd of buffalo, raising their halberds and chopping off the heads of panic-stricken boys who could not even muster the courage to run. It was a wave of death, a wave of destruction.

The captain himself stood there on his tower, too terrified to do anything, to even draw his sword, as the trolls raced for him. A moment later he felt himself falling, as the angry mob knocked down his tower. He felt himself landing in the trolls' arms, and he shrieked as he felt himself grabbed by their claws, torn to pieces.

And as he lay there dying, knowing what was coming for Escalon, a final thought crossed his mind: the boy who was stabbed, who had died for the morsel of bread, was the luckiest of all.

CHAPTER TWO

Dierdre felt her lungs being crushed as she tumbled end over end, deep underwater, desperate for air. She tried to get her bearings but was unable, thrown around by the massive waves of water, her world turning upside down again and again. She wanted more than anything to take a deep breath, her entire body screaming for oxygen, yet she knew that to do so would certainly mean her death.

She closed her eyes and cried, her tears merging with the water, wondering if this hell would ever end. Her only solace came in thinking of Marco. She had seen him, with her, tumbling in the waters, had felt him holding her hand, and she turned and searched for him. Yet as she looked, she saw nothing, nothing but blackness and waves of foaming, crushing water driving her down. Marco, she assumed, was long dead.

Dierdre wanted to cry, yet the pain knocked any thoughts of self-pity from her mind, made her think only of survival. For just when she thought the wave could not get any stronger, it smashed her down into the ground, again and again, pinning her down with such force that she felt as if the entire weight of the world were atop her. She knew she would not survive.

How ironic, she thought, to die here, in her home city, crushed beneath a tidal wave created by Pandesians' cannon fire. She would rather have died any other way. She could, she thought, handle almost any form of death—except for drowning. She couldn't take this awful pain, the flailing, being unable to open her mouth and take that one breath that every ounce of her body so desperately craved.

She felt herself getting weaker, giving in to the pain—and then, just as she felt her eyes about to close, just as she knew she could not stand it one second longer, she suddenly felt herself turning, spinning rapidly upward, the wave shooting her up with the same force that it had used to crush her. She rose upward with the momentum of a catapult, racing for the surface, the sunlight visible, the pressure killing her ears.

To her shock, a moment later she surfaced. She gasped, taking huge gulps of air, more grateful than she had ever been in her life. She gasped, sucking it in, and then a moment later, to her terror, she was sucked back down underwater. This time, though, she had enough oxygen to survive a little longer, and this time the water didn't push her down as far.

She soon rose back up again, surfacing, taking another gasp of air, before being driven down yet again. It was different each time, the wave weakening, and as she surfaced again, she sensed the wave was reaching the end of the city and petering out.

Dierdre soon found herself past the city limits, past all the great buildings, all of them now underwater. She was driven back underwater, yet slow enough to be able to finally open her eyes underwater and see all the grand buildings beneath that had once stood. She saw scores of corpses floating in the water past her, like fish, bodies whose death expressions she already tried to drive from her mind.

Finally, she did not know how much later, Dierdre surfaced, this time for good. She was strong enough to fight the final, weak wave as it tried to suck her back down, and with one last kick, she stayed afloat. The water from the harbor had traveled too far inland, and there was nowhere left for it to go, and Dierdre soon felt herself washed up onto a grassy field somewhere as the waters receded, rushing back out to sea, leaving her alone.

Dierdre lay there on her stomach, face planted in the soggy grass, moaning from the pain. She was still gasping, her lungs aching, breathing deep and savoring every breath. She managed to turn her head weakly, to look back over her shoulder, and she was horrified to see that what had once been a great city was now nothing but sea. She spotted only the highest part of the bell tower, sticking out a few feet, and marveled that it once stood hundreds of feet in the air.

Beyond exhausted, Dierdre finally let herself go. Her face fell to the ground as she lay there, letting the pain of what had happened overcome her. She couldn't move if she tried.

Moments later she was fast asleep, barely alive on a remote field in a corner of the world. Yet somehow, she was alive.

*

"Dierdre," came a voice, and a gentle nudge.

Dierdre peeled open her eyes, dazed to see it was sunset. Icy cold, her clothes still wet, she tried to get her bearings, wondering how long she had been lying here, wondering if she were alive or dead. Then the hand came again, nudging her shoulder.

Dierdre looked up and there, to her immense relief, was Marco. He was alive, she was overjoyed to see. He looked beaten up, haggard, too pale, and he looked as if he had aged a hundred years. Yet he was alive. Somehow, he had managed to survive.

Marco knelt beside her, smiling yet looking down at her with sad eyes, eyes not shining with the life they once held.

"Marco," she answered weakly, startled at how raspy her own voice was.

She noticed a gash on the side of his face and, concerned, reached out to touch it.

"You look as bad as I feel," she said.

He helped her up and she rose to her feet, her body wracked with pain from all the aches and bruises, scratches and cuts all up and down her arms and legs. Yet as she tested each limb, at least nothing was broken.

Dierdre took a deep breath and steeled herself as she turned and looked behind her. As she feared, it was a nightmare: her beloved city was gone, now nothing but a part of the sea, the only thing sticking up a small part of the bell tower. On the horizon beyond it she saw a fleet of black Pandesian ships, making their way deeper and deeper inland.

"We can't stay here," Marco said with urgency. "They're coming."

"Where can we go?" she asked, feeling hopeless.

Marco stared back, blank, clearly not knowing either.

Dierdre stared out at the sunset, trying to think, blood pounding in her ears. Everyone she knew and loved was dead. She felt she had nothing left to live for, nowhere left to go. Where could you go when your home city was destroyed? When the weight of the world was bearing down on you?

Dierdre closed her eyes and shook her head in grief, wishing it all away. Her father, she knew, was back there, dead. His soldiers were all dead. People she had known and loved all her life, all of them dead, all thanks to these Pandesian monsters. Now there was no one left to stop them. What cause was there to go on?

Dierdre, despite herself, broke down weeping. Thinking of her father, she dropped to her knees, feeling devastated. She wept and wept, wanting to die here herself, wishing she *had* died, cursing the heavens for allowing her to live. Why couldn't she have just drowned in that wave? Why couldn't she just have been killed with the others? Why had she been cursed with life?

She felt a soothing hand on her shoulder.

"It's okay, Dierdre," Marco said softly.

Dierdre flinched, embarrassed.

"I'm sorry," she finally said, weeping. "It's just that… my father… Now I have nothing."

"You've lost everything," Marco said, his voice heavy, too. "I have, too. I don't want to go on, either. But we *have* to. We can't lie here and die. It would dishonor them. It would dishonor everything they lived and fought for."

In the long silence that followed, Dierdre slowly pulled herself upright, realizing he was right. Besides, as she looked up at Marco's brown eyes, staring back at her with compassion, she realized she *did* have someone. She had Marco. She also had the spirit of her father, looking down, watching over her, wishing her to be strong.

She forced herself to shake out of it. She had to be strong. Her father would want her to be strong. Self-pity, she realized, would help no one. And neither would her death.

She stared back at Marco, and she could see more than compassion—she could also see the love in his eyes for her.

Not even fully aware of what she was doing, Dierdre, her heart pounding, leaned in and met Marco's lips in an unexpected kiss. For a moment, she felt herself transported to another world, and all her worries disappeared.

She slowly pulled back, staring at him, shocked. Marco looked equally surprised. He took her hand.

As he did, encouraged, filled with hope, she was able to think clearly again—and a thought came to her. There was someone else, a place to go, a person to turn to.

Kyra.

Dierdre felt a sudden rush of hope.

"I know where we must go," she said excitedly, in a rush.

Marco looked at her, wondering.

7

"Kyra," she said. "We can find her. She will help us. Wherever she is, she is fighting. We can join her."

"But how do you know she is alive?" he asked.

Dierdre shook her head.

"I don't," she replied. "But Kyra always survives. She is the strongest person I have ever met."

"Where is she?" he asked.

Dierdre thought, and she recalled the last time she had seen Kyra, forking north, for the Tower.

"The Tower of Ur," she said.

Marco looked back, surprised; then a glimmer of optimism crossed his eyes.

"The Watchers are there," he said. "As are other warriors. Men who can fight with us." He nodded, excited. "A good choice," he added. "We can be safe in that tower. And if your friend is there, then all the better. It's a day's hike from here. Let us go. We must move quickly."

He took her hand, and without another word the two of them took off, Dierdre filled with a new sense of optimism as they headed into the forest, and somewhere, on the horizon, for the Tower of Ur.

CHAPTER THREE

Kyra braced herself as she walked into a field of fire. The flames rose to the sky then lowered just as quickly, turning all different colors, caressing her as she walked with her arms out by her sides. She felt its intensity, felt it enveloping her, wrapping her in a thin embrace. She knew she was walking into death, and yet she could walk no other way.

And yet somehow, incredibly, she did not feel pain. She felt a sense of peace. A sense of her life ending.

She looked out and through the flames, she saw her mother, awaiting her somewhere at the far end, on the opposite side of the field. She felt a sense of peace, as she finally knew she would be in her mother's embrace.

I'm here, Kyra, she called. *Come to me.*

Kyra peered into the flames and could just make out her mother's face, nearly translucent, partially hidden as a wall of flame shot up. She walked deeper into the crackling flames, unable to stop until she was surrounded on all sides.

A roar cut through the air, even above the sound of the fire, and she looked up and was in awe to see a sky filled with dragons. They circled and shrieked, and as she watched, one huge dragon roared and dove down just for her.

Kyra sensed it was death coming for her.

As the dragon neared, its talons extended, suddenly the ground dropped out beneath her and Kyra found herself falling, hurtling down into the earth, an earth filled with flame, a place from which she knew she would never escape.

Kyra opened her eyes with a start, breathing hard. She looked all around, wondering where she was, feeling pain in every corner of her body. She felt the pain in her face, her cheek swollen, throbbing, and as she slowly lifted her head, finding it hard to breathe, she found that her face was encased in mud. She was, she realized, lying face first in the mud, and as she placed her palms in it and slowly pushed up, she wiped mud back from her face, wondering what was happening.

A sudden roar ripped through the air, and Kyra looked up and felt a wave of terror as she spotted something in the sky that was very real. The air was filled with dragons of all shapes and sizes and colors, all circling, screeching, breathing fire into the air, filled with fury. As she watched, one swooped down and breathed a column of flame all the way to the ground.

Kyra looked over and took in her surroundings, and her heart skipped a beat as she realized where she was: Andros.

It all came rushing back to her. She had been flying atop Theon, racing back to Andros to save her father, when they had been attacked in the sky by that flock of dragons. They had appeared from nowhere in the sky, had bitten Theon, had thrown them down to the ground. Kyra realized she must have blacked out.

Now she woke to a wave of heat, of awful shrieking, of a capital in chaos, and she looked about and saw the capital aflame. Everywhere, people were running for their lives, shrieking, as fire descended in waves, like a storm. It looked as if the end of the world had come.

Kyra heard labored breathing, and her heart fell to see Theon lying close by, on his side, wounded, blood pouring from his scales. His eyes were closed, his tongue hanging out the side of his mouth, and he looked on the verge of death. The only reason they were still alive, she realized, was that she and Theon were covered in a mound of rubble. They must have been thrown into a building, which collapsed on top of them. At least that had kept them sheltered, out of view of the dragons high above.

Kyra knew she had to get herself and Theon out of there at once. They hadn't much time until they were spotted.

"Theon!" she urged.

She turned and heaved, crushed by the rubble, and finally managed to shove a huge piece of rubble off her back, freeing herself. She then hurried over to Theon and frantically shoved at the mound of rubble atop him. She was able to push off most of the rocks, yet as she shoved at the large boulder on his back, pinning him down, she got nowhere. She shoved again and again, yet no matter how hard she tried, it would not budge.

Kyra ran over and grabbed Theon's face, desperate to rouse him. She stroked his scales, and slowly, to her relief, Theon opened his eyes. Yet he then closed his eyes again, as she shook him harder.

"Wake up!" Kyra demanded. "I need you!"

Theon's eyes opened again, slightly, then turned and looked over at her. The pain and fury in his eyes softened as he recognized her. He tried to shift, to get up, but clearly he was too weak; the boulder pinned him down.

Kyra shoved the boulder furiously, yet she broke down crying as she realized they could not get it to move. Theon was stuck. He would die here. And so would she.

Kyra, hearing a roar, looked up and saw a massive dragon with spiked green scales had spotted them. It roared with fury, then began to dive right for them.

Leave me.

Kyra heard a voice reverberating deep inside her. Theon's voice.

Hide. Go far from here. While there is still time.

"No!" she cried, shaking, refusing to leave him.

Go, he urged. *Or else we will both die here.*

"Then we shall both die!" she cried, a steely determination overtaking her. She would not abandon her friend. Not ever.

The sky darkened and Kyra looked up to see the huge dragon diving down, talons extended. It opened its mouth, rows of sharpened teeth showing, and she knew she would not survive. But she did not care. She would not abandon Theon. Death would take her. But not cowardice. She did not fear dying. Only not living well.

CHAPTER FOUR

Duncan ran with the others through the streets of Andros, hobbling, trying his best to keep pace with Aidan, Motley, and the young girl with them, Cassandra, while Aidan's dog, White, nipped at his heels and urged him on. Dragging his arm was his old and trusted commander, Anvin, his new squire Septin by his side, trying his best to keep him moving, yet clearly in bad shape himself. Duncan could see how injured his friend was, and it moved him that he had come in this state, had risked his life and traveled all this way to free him.

The ragtag group sprinted down the war-torn streets of Andros, chaos erupting all around them, all the odds against them for survival. On the one hand, Duncan felt so relieved to be free, so happy to see his son again, so grateful to be with all of them. Yet as he searched the skies, he also sensed he had left a jail cell only to be thrown into a sure death. The sky was filled with circling dragons, swooping down, swiping buildings, destroying the city as they breathed their awful columns of flame. Entire streets were filled with fire, blocking off the group's every turn. As one street at a time was lost, escape from the capital seemed less and less likely.

Motley clearly knew these back alleys well, and he led them deftly, turning down one alley after another, finding shortcuts everywhere, managing to avoid the roving packs of Pandesian soldiers, which was the other threat to their escape. Yet Motley, for all his craftiness, could not avoid the dragons, and as he turned them down another alley, it, too, was suddenly aflame. They all stopped in their tracks, faces burning from the heat, and retreated.

Duncan, covered in sweat as he backed up, looked to Motley, and he took no solace as, this time, Motley turned every which way, his face etched in panic.

"This way!" Motley finally said.

He turned and led them down another side alley, and they ducked beneath a stone arch right before a dragon filled the spot they had just stood with a fresh wave of fire.

As they ran, it pained Duncan to see this great city torn apart, this place he had once loved and defended. He could not help but feel as if Escalon would never be returned to its former glory. That his homeland was ruined forever.

There came a shout, and Duncan glanced back over his shoulder to see dozens of Pandesian soldiers had spotted them. They were chasing them down the alley, closing in, and Duncan knew they could not fight them—and could not outrun them. The exit to the city was still far, and their time had run out.

There suddenly came a great crash—and Duncan looked up to see a dragon swipe the bell tower off the castle with its talons.

"Look out!" he yelled.

He lunged forward and knocked Aidan and the others out of the way right before the remnants of the tower crashed beside them. A huge chunk of stone landed behind him with a deafening crash, raising up a pile of dust.

Aidan looked up at his father, shock and gratitude in his eyes, and Duncan felt a sense of satisfaction that he had at least saved his son's life.

Duncan heard the muffled shouts, and he turned and realized, with gratitude, that the rubble had at least blocked the way of the pursuing soldiers.

They kept running, Duncan struggling to keep up, his weakness and injuries from his imprisonment gnawing away at him; he was still malnourished, bruised, and beaten, and each step was a painful effort. Yet he forced himself to go on, if for no other reason than to make sure his son and his friends survived. He could not let them down.

They turned a narrow corner and reached a fork in the alleyways. They paused, all looking to Motley.

"We have to get out of this city!" Cassandra yelled to Motley, clearly frustrated. "And you don't even know where you're going!"

Motley looked left, then right, clearly stumped.

"There used to be a brothel down this alley," he said, looking to his right. "It leads out the back of the city."

"A brothel?" Cassandra retorted. "Nice company that you keep."

"I don't care what company you keep," Anvin added, "as long as it gets us out of here."

"Let's just hope it's not blocked," Aidan added.

"Let's go!" Duncan called out.

Motley began to run again, turning right, out of shape and gasping for breath.

They turned and followed, all putting their hope in Motley as he ran through the deserted back alleys of the capital.

They turned again and again, and finally, they came upon a low stone archway. They all ducked, running through it, and as they emerged from the other side, Duncan was relieved to find it open up. He was thrilled to see, in the distance, the rear gate of Andros, and the open plains and desert beyond it. Just beyond the gate stood dozens of Pandesian horses, tied up, clearly abandoned by their dead riders.

Motley grinned.

"I told you," he said.

Duncan ran with the others, gaining speed, feeling returned to his old self again, feeling a whole new rush of hope—when suddenly, there came a cry that pierced his soul.

He stopped short, listening.

"Wait!" he called out to the others.

They all stopped and looked back at him as if he were mad.

Duncan stood there, waiting. Could it be? He could have sworn he had heard the voice of his daughter. Kyra. Was he hearing things?

Of course, he must have imagined it. How could she possibly be *here*, in Andros? She was far from here, across Escalon, in the Tower of Ur, safe and sound.

Yet he could not bring himself to leave after hearing it.

He stood there, frozen, waiting—and then, he heard it again. His hair stood on end. He was sure this time. It was Kyra.

"Kyra!" he said aloud, his eyes widening.

Without thinking, he turned his back on the others, turned his back on the exit, and ran back into the flaming city.

"Where are you going!?" Motley called out behind him.

"Kyra is here!" he called, still running. "And she's in danger!"

"Are you mad?" Motley said, rushing up and grabbing his shoulder. "You run back to a certain death!"

But Duncan, determined, shoved Motley's hand away and continued to run.

"A certain death," he replied, "would be turning my back on the daughter I love."

Duncan did not pause as he turned down an alleyway alone, sprinting back into death, into a city aflame. He knew it would mean his death. And he did not care. As long as he could see Kyra again.

Kyra, he thought. *Wait for me.*

CHAPTER FIVE

The Most Holy and Supreme Ra sat on his golden throne in the capital, in the midst of Andros, looked down on the chamber filled with his generals, slaves, and supplicants, and rubbed his palms into the throne's arms, burning with dissatisfaction. He knew he should feel victorious, sated, after all he had achieved. After all, Escalon had been the last holdout of freedom in the world, the last place in his empire not completely under his subjugation, and in the last few days he had managed to lead his forces through one of his great routs of all time. He closed his eyes and smiled, relishing the image of running over the Southern Gate, unimpeded, of razing all the cities in southern Escalon, of blazing a trail north, all the way to the capital. He grinned as he reflected that this country, once so bountiful, was now a massive grave.

In the north, Escalon, he knew, fared no better. His fleets had managed to flood the great city of Ur, now but a memory. On the eastern coast, his fleets had taken the Sea of Tears and destroyed all the port cities along the coast, beginning with Esephus. Hardly an inch of Escalon lay out of his grasp.

Most of all, Escalon's defiant commander, the rabble-rouser who had started all of this, Duncan, lay in a dungeon as Ra's captive. Indeed, as Ra looked out and watched the sun rise through the window, he was giddy with excitement at the idea of personally walking Duncan to the gallows. He would personally pull the cord and watch him die. He smiled at the thought. Today would be a beautiful day.

Ra's victory was complete on all fronts—and yet, still, he did not feel sated. Ra sat there and looked deep within himself, trying to understand this feeling of dissatisfaction. He had everything he wanted. What was nagging at him?

Ra had never felt sated, not in any of his campaigns, not his entire life. There had always been something burning in him, a desire for more, and more. Even now, he could feel it. What else could he do to fulfill his desires? he wondered. To make his victory truly feel complete?

Slowly, a plan came to him. He could murder every man, woman, and child left in Escalon. He could rape the women and torture the men first. He smiled wide. Yes, that would help. In fact, he could start right now.

Ra looked down at his advisors, hundreds of his best men, all kneeling before him, heads lowered, none daring to make eye contact. They all stared at the ground soundlessly, as they should. After all, they were lucky to be in the presence of a god such as himself.

Ra cleared his throat.

"Bring me the ten most beautiful women left in the land of Escalon at once," he commanded, his deep voice booming across the chamber.

One of his servants bowed his head until it touched the marble floor.

"Yes, my lord!" he said, as he turned and ran off.

Yet as the servant reached the door it slammed open first, as another servant burst into the chamber, frantic, running right toward Ra's throne. All the others in the room gasped, horrified by the affront. No one dared to ever enter a room, much less approach Ra, without a formal invitation. Doing so meant a certain death.

The servant threw himself face-first on the floor, and Ra glared down in disgust.

"Kill him," he commanded.

Immediately, several of his soldiers rushed forward and grabbed the man. They dragged him away, flailing, and as they did, he cried: "Wait, my awesome Lord! I come bearing urgent news—news you must hear at once!"

Ra let the man be dragged away, not caring for the news. The man flailed the entire way, until finally as he reached the exit, the door about to close, he yelled:

"Duncan has escaped!"

Ra, feeling a jolt of shock, suddenly raised his right palm. His men stopped, holding the messenger at the door.

Scowling, Ra slowly processed the news. He stood and breathed deep. He descended the ivory steps, one at a time, his golden boots echoing, as he crossed the entire chamber. The room was silent, filled with tension, as he finally stopped right before the messenger. With every step he took, Ra could feel his fury rising within him.

"Tell me again," Ra commanded, his voice dark and ominous.

The messenger shook.

"I am most sorry, my great and holy Supreme Lord," he said with a shaking voice, "but Duncan has fled. Someone has broken him out of the dungeons. Our men are pursuing him through the capital even as we speak!"

Ra felt his face flush, felt the fire burning within him. He clenched his fists. He would not allow it. He would not allow himself to be robbed of his final piece of satisfaction.

"Thank you for bringing me this news," Ra said.

Ra smiled, and for a moment the messenger looked relaxed, even began to smile back, puffing himself up with pride.

Ra *did* reward him. He stepped forward and slowly wrapped his hands around the man's neck, then squeezed and squeezed. The man's eyes bulged in his head and he reached up and grabbed Ra's wrists—but was unable to pull them off. Ra knew he would not be able to. After all, he was just a man, and Ra was the great and holy Ra, the Man Who Was Once a God.

The man collapsed to the floor, dead. Yet it still gave Ra little satisfaction.

"Men!" Ra boomed.

His commanders snapped to attention and looked back with fear.

"Block every exit to the city! Dispatch every soldier we have to find this Duncan. And while you're at it, kill every last man, woman, and child inside the city of Escalon. GO!"

"Yes, Supreme Lord!" the men replied, as one.

They all raced from the room, stumbling over each other, each rushing to do their master's bidding faster than the others.

Ra turned, seething, and took a deep breath as he crossed the now empty chamber alone. He exited out to a broad balcony overlooking the city.

Ra stepped outside and felt the fresh air as he surveyed the chaotic city below. His soldiers, he was happy to see, occupied most of it. He wondered where Duncan could be. He admired him, he had to give him that; perhaps he even saw something of himself in him. Still, Duncan would learn what it meant to cross the great Ra. He would learn to accept death graciously. He would learn to submit, like the rest of the world.

Cries began to ring out, and Ra looked down and saw his men raising swords and spears and stabbing unsuspecting men and women and children in the back. Per his orders, the streets began to flow with blood. Ra sighed, contenting himself in this, and taking some satisfaction in it. All of these Escalonites would learn. It was the same everywhere he went, in every country he conquered. They would pay for their commander's sins.

A sudden noise cut through the air, though, even above the cries below, startling Ra from his reverie. He could not understand what it was, or why it disturbed him so much. It was a low, deep rumble, something like thunder.

Just as he wondered if he had really heard it, it came again, louder, and he realized it was not coming from the ground—but from the sky.

Ra looked up, baffled, peering into the clouds, wondering. The sound came again, and again, and he knew it was not thunder. It was something much more ominous.

As he examined the rolling, gray clouds, Ra suddenly saw a sight that he would never forget. He blinked, certain he was imagining it. But no matter how many times he looked away, it was still there.

Dragons. An entire flock.

They descended for Escalon, talons extended, wings raised, breathing flames of fire. And flying right for him.

Before he could even process it, hundreds of his soldiers below were set aflame by the dragons' breath, shrieking, caught in the columns of fire. Hundreds more groaned as the dragons tore them to shreds.

As he stood there, numb with panic, with disbelief, an enormous dragon singled him out. It aimed for his balcony, raised its talons, and dove.

A moment later, it sliced the stone in half, just missing him as he ducked. Ra, in a panic, felt the stone give way beneath his feet.

Moments later he felt himself falling, flailing, shrieking, down for the ground below. He had thought he was untouchable, greater than them all.

Yet death, after all, had found him.

CHAPTER SIX

Kyle swung his staff with all he had, reeling from exhaustion as he struck both the Pandesian soldiers and the trolls closing in on him from all sides. He felled men and trolls left and right as their swords and halberds clanged off his staff, sparks flying everywhere. Even while defeating them, he could feel the ache, deep in his shoulders. He had been battling them for hours, he was surrounded on all sides now, and his situation, he knew, was dire.

At first the Pandesians and trolls had fought each other, leaving him free to fight whom he wished, yet as they saw Kyle felling everyone around him, they clearly realized it was in their best interest to team up against him. For a moment the Pandesians and trolls had stopped trying to kill each other, and instead all focused on killing him.

As Kyle swung and knocked back three trolls, a Pandesian managed to sneak behind him and slash Kyle's stomach with his sword. Kyle shouted out and reeled from the pain, spinning to avoid the worst of it, yet still bleeding. Before he could parry, at the same time, a troll raised a club and smashed Kyle in the shoulder, knocking the staff from his hand and sending him to his hands and knees.

Kyle knelt there, the pain shooting up and down his shoulder, throbbing, as he tried to catch his breath. Before he could gather himself, yet another troll rushed forward and kicked him in the face, sending him flat on his back.

A Pandesian then stepped forward with a long spear, raised it high with both hands, and brought it down for Kyle's head.

Kyle, not ready to die, spun out of the way, and the spear planted itself in the ground just inches from his face. He continued to roll, gained his feet, and as two more trolls charged, he grabbed a sword from the ground, spun, and stabbed them both.

As several others crowded in, Kyle quickly grabbed his staff and knocked them all out, fighting like a cornered animal as he formed a circle around him. He stood there, breathing heavily, blood pouring from his lip, while his opponents formed a thick circle around him, all closing in, blood in their eyes.

The pain in his stomach and shoulder unbearable, Kyle tried to block it out, tried to focus as he stood there. He faced an imminent death, he knew, and he took solace only in the fact that he had rescued Kyra. That had made it all worth it, and he was willing to pay the price.

He glanced at the horizon, and took solace in the fact that she had gotten away from all this, had ridden away on the back of Andor. He wondered if she was safe, and prayed that she was.

Kyle had fought brilliantly, for hours, one man up against both these armies, and had killed thousands of them. Yet now, he knew, he was too weak to go on. There were just too many of them, and their numbers never seemed to end. He had found himself in the middle of a war, the trolls flooding the land from the north while the Pandesians streamed up from the South, and he could no longer fight them both.

Kyle felt a sudden pain in his ribs as a troll rushed him from behind and jabbed him in the back with the shaft of his ax. Kyle swung around with his staff, slashing the troll in the throat, dropping him—but at the same time two Pandesian soldiers rushed forward and smashed him with their shields. The pain in his head overwhelming, Kyle dropped down to the ground, this time, he knew, for good. He was too weak to rise again.

Kyle closed his eyes and there flashed through his mind images of his life. He saw all the Watchers, people he had served with for centuries, saw all the people he had known and loved. Most of all, he saw Kyra's face. The only thing he regretted was that he would not see her again before he died.

Kyle looked up as three hideous trolls stepped forward, raising their halberds. He knew this was it.

As they began to lower them, everything came into focus. He was able to hear the sound of the wind; to really smell the crisp, cool air. For the first time in centuries, he felt truly alive. He wondered why he had never been able to truly appreciate life until he was almost dead.

As Kyle closed eyes and braced himself for death's embrace, suddenly a roar pierced the sky. It snapped him from his reverie. He blinked and glanced up to see something emerge through the clouds. At first Kyle thought it was angels, coming to take away his dead body.

But then he saw that the trolls above him were frozen in confusion themselves, all searching the sky—and Kyle knew it was real. It was something else.

And then, as he caught a glimpse of what it was, his heart stopped.

Dragons.

A flock of dragons circled, diving down in fury, breathing fire. They descended rapidly, talons extended, letting loose their flame and, without warning, killing hundreds of soldiers and trolls at once. A wave of fire rolled down, spreading, and within seconds, the trolls standing over Kyle were all burnt to a crisp. Kyle, seeing the flames coming, grabbed a huge copper shield beside him and took shelter behind it, curling up in a ball. The heat was intense as the flames rolled off it, nearly burning his hands, yet he held on. The dead trolls and soldiers landed on top of him, their armor further shielding him as yet another wave of flame came, this one more powerful. Ironically, these trolls and Pandesians were now saving him from death.

He held on, sweating, barely able to stand the heat as the dragons dove again and again. Unable to stand it any longer, he passed out, praying with all he was that he was not burned alive.

CHAPTER SEVEN

Vesuvius stood at the edge of the cliff, beside the Tower of Kos, staring down at the crashing waves of the Sorrow, the steam still rising from where the Sword of Fire had sunk—and he grinned wide. He had done it. The Sword of Flames was no more. He had robbed the Tower of Kos, had robbed Escalon, of its most precious artifact. He had, once and for all time, lowered the Flames.

Vesuvius beamed, giddy with excitement. His palm still throbbed from where he had grabbed the burning Sword of Flames, and he looked down and saw the insignia branded in it. He ran his finger along his fresh scars, knowing they would stay there forever, a mark of his success. The pain was blinding, yet he forced it from his mind, forced it not to bother him. In fact, he taught himself to enjoy the pain.

After all these centuries, now, finally, his people would have their due. No longer would they be relegated to Marda, to the northernmost reaches of the empire, to infertile land. Now they would take their vengeance for being quarantined behind a wall of flames, would flood Escalon, tear it to shreds.

His heart skipped a beat, giddy at the thought. He could not wait to turn back around, to cross the Devil's Finger, to return to the mainland and to meet his people in the middle of Escalon. The entire troll nation would converge at Andros, and together, one square inch at a time, they would destroy Escalon forever. It would become the new troll homeland.

Yet as Vesuvius stood there, looking down at the waves, the spot where the sword had sunk, something gnawed at him. He looked out to the horizon, examining the black waters of the Bay of Death, and there was something lingering, something that made his satisfaction incomplete. As he examined the horizon, far out in the distance, he spotted a single, small ship with white sails, sailing along the Bay of Death. It sailed west, away from the Devil's Finger. And as he watched it go, he knew something was wrong.

Vesuvius turned back and looked up at the Tower beside him. It had been empty. Its doors left open. The Sword had been waiting for him. Those guarding had abandoned it. It had all been too easy.

Why?

Vesuvius knew the assassin Merk had been pursuing the Sword; he had followed him all the way across the Devil's Finger. Why then would he abandon it? Why was he sailing away from here, across the Bay of Death? Who was that woman sailing with him? Had she been guarding this tower? What secrets was she hiding?

And where were they going?

Vesuvius looked down at the steam rising from the ocean, then back up to the horizon, and his veins burned. He could not help but feel that somehow he had been duped. That a complete victory had been snatched from him.

The more Vesuvius dwelled on it, the more he realized something was wrong. It was all too convenient. He studied the violent seas below, the waves crashing into the rocks, the rising steam, and he realized he would never know the truth. He would never know if the Sword of Flames had truly sunk to the bottom. If there was something here he was missing. If that had even been the right sword. If the Flames would stay down, too.

Vesuvius, burning with indignation, came to a decision: he had to pursue them. He would never know the truth until he did. Was there another, secret, tower somewhere? Another sword?

Even if there was not, even if he had accomplished all he needed, Vesuvius was famed for leaving no victims alive. Ever. He always pursued every last man to his death, and standing here, watching those two escape from his grasp, did not sit right with him. He knew he could not just let them go.

Vesuvius looked down at the dozens of ships still tied to the shores, abandoned, rocking wildly in the waves, as if waiting for him. And he came to an immediate decision.

"To the ships!" he commanded his army of trolls.

As one they scrambled to do his bidding, rushing down to the rocky shore, boarding the ships. Vesuvius followed, boarding the stern of the final ship.

He turned, raised his halberd high, and chopped the rope.

A moment later he was off, all the trolls with him, all of them crammed onto ships, and setting sail on the legendary Bay of Death. Somewhere on the horizon sailed Merk and that girl. And Vesuvius would not stop, no matter where he had to sail, until both of them were dead.

CHAPTER EIGHT

Merk gripped the rail as he stood at the bow of the small ship, the former King Tarnis's daughter beside him, each lost in their own world as they were thrown about by the rough waters of the Bay of Death. Merk stared out at the black waters, windswept, dotted with whitecaps, and he could not help but wonder about the woman beside him. The mystery surrounding her had only deepened since they'd left the Tower of Kos, had embarked on this ship to some mysterious place. His mind swam with questions for her.

Tarnis's daughter. It was hard for Merk to believe. What had she been doing out here, at the end of the Devil's Finger, holed up in the Tower of Kos? Was she in hiding? In exile? Being protected? From whom?

Merk sensed that she, with her translucent eyes, her too-pale complexion and unflappable poise, was of another race. But if so, then who was her mother? Why had she been left alone to guard the Sword of Flames, the Tower of Kos? Where had all her people gone?

And most pressing of all, where was she leading them now?

One hand on the rudder, she steered the ship deeper into the bay, to some destination on the horizon that Merk could only wonder at.

"You still haven't told me where we're going," he said, raising his voice to be heard over the wind.

There followed a long silence, so long, he was unsure if she would ever reply.

"At least, then, tell me your name," he added, realizing she had never offered it.

"Lorna," she replied.

Lorna. He liked the sound of it.

"The Three Daggers," she added, turning to him. "That's where we're going."

Merk frowned.

"The Three Daggers?" he asked, surprised.

She merely looked straight ahead.

Merk, though, was stunned by the news. The most remote islands in all of Escalon, The Three Daggers were so deep in the Bay of Death, he had not known of anyone who had ever actually traveled there. Knossos, of course, the legendary isle and fort, sat on the last of them, and legend had always had it that it held Escalon's fiercest warriors. They were men who lived on a desolate island off a desolate peninsula, in the most dangerous body of water there was. They were men rumored to be as rough as the sea that surrounded them. Merk had never met one in person. No one had. They were more legend than real.

"Did your Watchers retreat there?" he asked.

Lorna nodded.

"They await us now," she said.

Merk turned and looked back over his shoulder, wanting one last glimpse of the Tower of Kos, and as he did, his heart suddenly stopped at what he saw: there, on the horizon, pursuing them, were dozens of ships, sails full.

"We've got company," he said.

Lorna, to his surprise, did not even turn around, but merely nodded.

"They will chase us to the ends of the earth," she said calmly.

Merk was puzzled.

"Even though they have the Sword of Flames?"

"It was never the Sword that they were after," she corrected. "It was destruction. The destruction of us all."

"And when they catch us?" Merk asked. "We cannot fight off an army of trolls alone. Nor can a small isle of warriors, no matter how tough they may be."

She nodded, still unfazed.

"We may indeed die," she replied. "Yet we shall do it in the company of our fellow Watchers, fighting for what we know is true. There are many secrets left to guard."

"Secrets?" he asked.

But she fell silent, watching the waters.

He was about to ask her more, when a sudden gale of wind nearly capsized the boat. Merk fell to his stomach, slamming into the side of the hull and sliding over the edge.

Dangling, he grasped onto the rail for dear life as his legs sank into the water, water so icy cold he felt he would freeze to death. He hung on with a single hand, mostly submerged, and as he looked back down over his shoulder, his heart leapt to see a school of red sharks suddenly closing in. He felt horrific pain as teeth began to dig into his calf, as he saw blood in the water that he knew was his own.

A moment later Lorna stepped forward and cracked the waters with her staff; as she did, brilliant white light spread on the surface, and the sharks dispersed. In the same motion she grabbed his hand and dragged him back onto the ship.

The ship righted itself as the wind subsided and Merk sat on deck, wet, freezing, breathing hard, and a terrible pain in his calf.

Lorna examined his wound, tore a piece of cloth from her shirt, and wrapped it around his leg, staunching the blood.

"You saved my life," he said, filled with gratitude. "There were dozens of those things in there. They would have killed me."

She looked him, her light blue eyes hypnotizing, so large.

"Those creatures are the least of your worries here," she said.

They sailed on in silence, Merk slowly regaining his feet and watching the horizon, sure to grip the rail tightly, with both hands this time. He examined the horizon, but as much as he watched it, he saw no sign of the Three Daggers. He looked down and studied the waters of the Bay of Death with a new respect and fear. He looked carefully, and saw swarms of small red sharks under the surface, barely visible, hidden mostly by the waves. He knew now that entering that water meant death—and he could not help but wonder what other creatures inhabited this body of water.

The silence deepened, punctuated only by the howling of the wind, and after hours more passed, Merk, feeling desolate out here, needed to talk.

"What you did what that staff," Merk said, turning to Lorna. "I have never seen anything like it."

Lorna remained expressionless, still watching the horizon.

"Tell me about you," he pressed.

She glanced at him, then looked back to the horizon.

"What would you like to know?" she asked.

"Anything," he replied. "Everything."

She fell silent a long time, then finally, she said:

"Start with you."

Merk stared back, surprised.

"Me?" he asked. "What do you want to know?"

"Tell me about your life," she said. "Anything you want to tell me."

Merk took a deep breath as he turned and stared into the horizon. His life was the one thing he did not want to talk about.

Finally, realizing they had a long journey ahead, he sighed. He knew he had to face himself at one time or another, even if he was not proud of it.

"I've been an assassin most my life," he said slowly, regretfully, staring into the horizon, his voice grave and filled with self-loathing. "I'm not proud of it. But I was the best at what I did. I was in demand by kings and queens. No one could rival my skills."

Merk fell into a long silence, trapped in memories of a life he regretted, memories he would rather not recall.

"And now?" she asked softly.

Merk was grateful to detect no judgment in her voice, as he usually did with others. He sighed.

"Now," he said, "it is not what I do anymore. It is not who I am anymore. I have vowed to renounce violence. To put my services to a cause. Yet, try as I do, I cannot seem to get away from it. Violence seems to find me. There is always, it seems, another cause."

"And what is your cause?" she asked.

He thought about that.

"My cause, initially, was to become a Watcher," he replied. "To devote myself to service. To guard the Tower of Ur, to protect the Sword of Flames. When that fell, I felt my cause was to reach the Tower of Kos, to save the sword."

He sighed.

"And yet now here we are, sailing through the Bay of Death, the Sword gone, the trolls following, and heading to a barren chain of islands," Lorna replied with a smile.

Merk frowned, unamused.

"I have lost my cause," he said. "I have lost my life's purpose. I do not know myself anymore. I do not know my direction."

Lorna nodded.

"That is a good place to be," she said. "A place of uncertainty is also a place of possibility."

Merk studied her, wondering. He was touched by her lack of condemnation. Anyone else who had heard his tale would vilify him.

"You do not judge me," he observed, shocked, "for who I am."

Lorna stared at him, her eyes so intense it was like staring into the moon.

"That was who you *were*," she corrected. "Not who you are now. How can I judge you for who you once were? I only judge the man standing before me."

Merk felt restored by her answer.

"And who am I now?" he asked, wanting to know the answer, unsure of it himself.

She stared at him.

"I see a fine warrior," she replied. "A selfless man. A man who wants to help others. And a man full of longing. I see a man who is lost. A man who has never known himself."

Merk pondered her words, and they resonated deep within him. He felt them all to be true. Too true.

A long silence fell between them, as their small ship bobbed up and down in the waters, slowly making its way west. Merk checked back and saw the troll fleet still on the horizon, still a good enough distance away.

"And you?" he finally asked. "You are Tarnis's daughter, are you not?"

She searched the horizon, her eyes aglow, and finally, she nodded.

"I am," she replied.

Merk was stunned to hear it.

"Then why were you here?" he asked.

She sighed.

"I have been hidden here since I was a young girl."

"But why?" he pressed.

She shrugged.

"I suppose it was too dangerous to keep me in the capital. People could not know I was the King's illegitimate daughter. It was safer here."

"Safer here?" he asked. "At the ends of the earth?"

"I was left with a secret to guard," she explained. "More important even than the kingdom of Escalon."

His heart pounded as he wondered what it could be.

"Will you tell me?" he asked.

But Lorna slowly turned and pointed ahead. Merk followed her gaze and there, on the horizon, the sun shone down on three barren islands, rising up from the ocean, the last one a fort of solid stone. It was the most desolate and yet beautiful place Merk had ever seen. A place distant enough to hold all the secrets of magic and power.

"Welcome," Lorna said, "to Knossos."

CHAPTER NINE

Duncan, alone, hobbling from the pain in his ankles and wrists, ran through the streets of Andros, ignoring the pain, spurred on by adrenaline as he thought of only one thing: saving Kyra. Her cry for help echoed in his mind, his soul, made him forget his injuries as he sprinted through the streets, sweating, toward the sound.

Duncan twisted and turned down Andros' narrow alleyways, knowing Kyra lay just beyond those thick stone walls. All around him the dragons dove, setting fire to street after street, the tremendous heat radiating off the walls, so hot that Duncan could feel it even on the far side of the stone. He hoped and prayed they did not descend to his alley—or else, he would be finished.

Despite the pain, Duncan did not stop. Nor did he turn around. He could not. Driven by a father's instinct, he physically could not go anywhere but toward the sound of his daughter. It crossed his mind that he was running to his death, losing any chance he'd have of escape, yet it did not slow him. His daughter was trapped, and that was all that mattered to him now.

"NO!" came the cry.

Duncan's hair stood on end. There it was again, her shriek, and his heart received a jolt at the sound. He sprinted faster, giving it all he had, turning down yet another alleyway.

Finally, as he turned again, he burst through a low, stone arch, and the sky opened before him.

Duncan found himself in an open courtyard, and as he stood at its edge, he was stunned at the sight before him. Flames filled the far side of the courtyard as dragons criss-crossed the air, breathing down, and beneath a stone ledge, barely shielded from all the fire, sat his daughter.

Kyra.

There she was, in the flesh, alive.

Even more shocking than seeing her here, alive, was seeing the baby dragon lying beside her. Duncan stared, confused by the sight. At first he assumed Kyra was struggling to kill a dragon that had fallen from the sky. But then he saw that the dragon was pinned down by a boulder. He was puzzled as he saw Kyra shoving at it. What, he wondered, was she trying to do? Free a dragon? Why?

"Kyra!" he shrieked.

Duncan sprinted across the open courtyard, avoiding columns of flame, avoiding the swipe of a dragon's talon, still running until finally he reached his daughter's side.

As he did, Kyra looked up and her face fell in shock. And then joy.

"Father!" she called.

She ran into his arms, and Duncan embraced her, as she embraced him back. As he held her in his arms, he felt restored again, as if a part of himself had returned.

Tears of joy ran down his cheeks. He could hardly believe Kyra was really here, and alive.

She clutched him and he clutched her, and he was relieved most of all, as he felt her shaking in his arms, that she was uninjured.

Remembering, he pushed her back, turned to the dragon, drew his sword, and raised it, about to chop off the dragon's head to protect his daughter.

"No!" Kyra shrieked.

She stunned Duncan by rushing forward and grabbing his wrist, her grip surprisingly strong, and holding back his blow. This was not the meek daughter he had left behind in Volis; she was clearly a warrior now.

Duncan looked back at her, baffled.

"Do not harm him," she commanded, her voice confident, the voice of a warrior. "Theon is my friend."

Duncan looked at her, stunned.

"Your *friend*?" he asked. "A dragon?"

"Please, Father," she said, "there is little time to explain. Help us. He is pinned down. I cannot remove this boulder alone."

Duncan, as shocked as he was, trusted her. He sheathed his sword, came up beside her, and pushed at the boulder with all his might. Yet, try as he did, it barely budged.

"It's too heavy," he said. "I can't. I am sorry."

Suddenly, there came the rattling of armor behind him and Duncan turned and was overjoyed to see Aidan, Anvin, Cassandra, and White all rush forward. They had come back for him, had risked their lives, too, once again.

Without hesitating, they all ran right up to the boulder and pushed.

It rolled a bit, but still they could not get it off.

There came the sound of gasping, and Duncan turned to see Motley rushing to catch up with the others, out of breath. He joined them, throwing his weight into the boulder—and this time, it began to really roll. Motley, the actor, the overweight fool, the one they had expected the least of, made the difference in getting the boulder off the dragon.

With one last heave it landed with a crash, in a cloud of dust, and the dragon was free.

Theon jumped to his feet and screeched, arching his back, extending his talons. In fury, he looked up at the sky. A big purple dragon had spotted them, was diving down right for them, and Theon, without pausing, leapt into the air, opened his jaws, and flew straight up, locking on the soft jugular of the unsuspecting dragon.

Theon held on with all his might. The huge dragon shrieked in fury, thrown off guard, clearly not expecting as much from the baby dragon, and the two of them went smashing down into a stone wall on the far side of the courtyard.

Duncan and the others exchanged a look of shock as Theon wrestled the dragon, refusing to let go of the squirming big dragon, pinning it down on the far side of the courtyard. Theon, ferocious, writhed, snarling, and did not let go until the much larger dragon finally went limp.

For a moment, they all had a respite.

"Kyra!" Aidan called out.

Kyra looked down and noticed her little brother, and Duncan watched with joy as Aidan ran into Kyra's arms. She embraced him, while White jumped up and licked Kyra's palms, clearly thrilled.

"My brother," Kyra gushed, her eyes filled with tears. "You are alive."

Duncan could hear the relief in her voice.

Aidan's eyes suddenly lowered in sadness.

"Brandon and Braxton are dead," he announced to Kyra.

Kyra paled. She turned and looked to Duncan, and he nodded in solemn confirmation.

Suddenly Theon flew up and landed before them, flapping his wings and gesturing for Kyra to climb on his back. Duncan heard the roars high above, and he looked up to see them all circling, preparing to dive.

To Duncan's awe, Kyra mounted Theon. There she sat, atop a dragon, strong, fierce, having all the poise of a great warrior. Gone was the little girl he had once known; she had been replaced by a proud warrior, a woman who could command legions. He had never felt more pride until this day.

"We have no time. Come with me," she said to them. "All of you. Join me."

They all looked at each other in surprise, and Duncan felt a pit in his stomach at the idea of riding a dragon, especially as it snarled down at them.

"Hurry!" she said.

Duncan, seeing the flock of dragons descending and knowing they had little choice, jumped into action. He hurried with Aidan, Anvin, Motley, Cassandra, Septin and White, as they all leapt onto the dragon's back.

He clutched the heavy, ancient scales, marveling that he was really sitting on the back of a dragon. It was like a dream.

He held on with all he had as the dragon lifted into the air. His stomach lightened, and he could hardly believe the feeling. For the first time in his life, he was flying in the air, above the streets, faster than he had ever been.

Theon, faster than them all, flew just above the streets, twisting and turning, so fast the other dragons could not reach him amidst all the confusion and dust of the capital. Duncan looked down and was amazed to see the city from above, to see the tops of buildings, the winding streets laid out like a maze below.

Kyra directed Theon brilliantly, and Duncan was so proud of his daughter, so amazed that she was able to control a beast like this. Within moments, they were free, in the open sky, beyond the capital walls, and soaring over the countryside.

"We must head south!" Anvin yelled out. "There are rock formations there, beyond the perimeter of the capital. All our men await us! They have retreated there."

Kyra directed Theon, and soon they were all flying south, toward a huge outcropping of rock on the horizon. Duncan saw up ahead the hundreds of massive boulders, dotted with small caves inside, on the horizon, south of the capital walls.

As they approached, Duncan saw the armor and weaponry inside the caves, glistening in the desert light, and his heart lifted to see hundreds of his men inside, awaiting him at this rallying point.

As Kyra directed Theon down, they landed at the entrance of a massive cave. Duncan could see the fear in the faces of the men below as the dragon approached, bracing themselves for an attack. But then they spotted Kyra and the others on his back, and their expressions changed to one of shock. They let down their guard.

Duncan dismounted with Kyra and the others, and he ran to embrace his men, overjoyed to see them alive again. There were Kavos and Bramthos, Seavig and Arthfael, men who'd risked their lives for him, men he thought he'd never see again.

Duncan turned and saw Kyra, and he was surprised to see she had not dismounted with the others.

"Why do you still sit there?" he asked. "Won't you join us?"

But Kyra sat there, her back so straight and proud, and solemnly shook her head.

"I mustn't, Father. I have some solemn business elsewhere. On behalf of Escalon."

Duncan stared back, baffled, marveling at the strong warrior his daughter had become.

"But where?" Duncan asked. "Where is more important than at our side?"

She hesitated.

"Marda," she replied.

Duncan felt a chill at the word.

"Marda?" he gasped. "You? Alone? You shall never return!"

She nodded, and he could see in her eyes that she already knew.

"I vowed to go," she replied, "and I cannot abandon my mission. Now that you are safe, my duty calls. Haven't you always taught me that duty comes first, Father?"

Duncan felt his heart swell with pride at her words. He stepped forward, reached up, and embraced her, clutching her to him as his men circled around.

"Kyra, my daughter. You are the better part of my soul."

He saw her eyes well with tears, and she nodded back, stronger, more powerful, without the sentiments she used to have. She gave a little kick, and Theon was quickly up in the air. Kyra flew proudly on his back, higher and higher, up in the sky.

Duncan's heart broke as he watched her go, heading north, wondering if he would ever see her again as she flew somewhere toward the blackness of Marda.

CHAPTER TEN

Kyra leaned forward and gripped Theon's scales as they flew, holding tight as the wind ripped through her hair. They flew in and out of clouds, her hands shaking from the moisture, the cold, yet Kyra ignored it all as they raced across Escalon on the way to Marda. Nothing would stop her now.

Kyra's mind swam with all she'd just been through, still trying to process it all. She recalled her father, and was happy to think of him safe with his men outside of Andros. She felt a great sense of satisfaction. Time and again she had almost died trying to reach him, had been warned to stay away at the cost of her life. Yet she had not given up, sensing deep in her heart that he needed her. She had learned a valuable lesson: she must always trust her instincts, no matter how many people warned her away.

Indeed, as she reflected on it, she realized now that that was precisely why Alva had warned her away: it was a test. He had made it clear that she would die if she went back for her father because he wanted to test her resolve, to test her courage. He had known all along that she would live. He wanted to see if she would head into battle, though, if she thought she would die.

Of course, at the same time her father had saved her; if he had not arrived when he had, Theon would still be pinned beneath that rubble and she would surely be dead. Thinking of her father sacrificing everything for her lifted her heart, too. It brought tears to her eyes as she thought of his braving the flames, and dragons, and death, all just for her.

Kyra smiled as she thought of her brother Aidan, so happy that he was alive and safe, too. She thought of her two dead brothers, and as much strife and rivalry as they'd had between them, it still pained her. She wished she could have been there to protect them.

Kyra thought of Andros, the once great capital, now a cauldron of flame, and her heart fell. Would Escalon ever return to its former glory?

So much had happened at once, Kyra could barely process it. It was as if the world were spinning out of control beneath her, as if the only constant these days was change.

Kyra tried to shake it all from her mind and focus on the journey before her: Marda. Kyra felt infused with a sense of purpose as she flew, her heart pounding, anxious to get there, to find the Staff of Truth. She dipped through clouds and looked down as she flew, looking for markers, trying see how close she was to the border, the Flames. As she searched the landscape, her heart fell to see what had become of her homeland: she saw a land torn apart, scarred, burnt by flames. She saw entire strongholds destroyed, whether by Pandesian soldiers, or marauding trolls, or enraged dragons, she did not know. She saw a land so ravaged it was unrecognizable from the place she had once known and loved. It was hard to believe. The Escalon she knew was no more.

It all felt surreal to her, hard to imagine that such change could come so drastically and so quickly. It made her wonder. What if, on that one snowy night, she had never encountered the wounded Theos? Would the fate of Escalon have taken a different course?

Or had it all been predestined? Was she the one responsible for all this, for all that she saw below? Or was she just the vehicle? Would it all have happened some other way regardless?

Kyra wanted so desperately to dive down, to land below, to stay here in Escalon and help wage war against the Pandesians, the trolls, to help fix whatever she could. Yet, despite a sense of looming dread, she forced herself to look up, to stay focused on her mission, to keep flying north, somewhere toward the blackness of Marda.

Kyra shivered. It would be a journey, she knew, to the very essence of darkness. Marda had always, since she had been young, been a place of legend, a place of such evil, so off limits, that no one would ever entertain the idea of visiting it. It was, on the contrary, a place to be sealed off from the world, to be protected from, a place that her people thanked the universe every day was shielded by the Flames. Now, unbelievably, a place she was seeking out.

On the one hand, it was madness. Yet on the other, Kyra's mother had sent her here, and she sensed deep down that the mission was true. She sensed that Marda was where she was needed, where her ultimate test lay. Where the Staff of Truth lay, that only she could retrieve. It was crazy, but she could already feel the staff, deep in her gut, summoning her, luring her to it like an old friend.

Still, Kyra, for the first time in as long as she could remember, felt a wave of self-doubt overwhelm her. Was she really strong enough to do this? To go to Marda, a place even her father's men feared to venture? She felt a battle raging within her own soul. Everything inside her screamed that to go to Marda would be to go to her death. And she did not want to die.

Kyra tried to force herself to be strong, not to veer from the path. She knew this was a journey she had to take, and she knew she could not shy away from what was demanded of her. She tried to push from her mind the horrors that awaited her on the far side of the Flames. A nation of trolls. Volcanoes, lava, ash. A nation of evil, of sorcery. Unimaginable creatures and monsters. She tried not to recall the stories she had heard as a child. A place where people tore each other apart for fun, led by the demonic leader Vesuvius. A nation that lived for blood, for cruelty.

They dipped down beneath the clouds for a moment, and Kyra glanced down and saw, far below, that they were passing over the northeastern corner of Escalon. Her heart leapt as she began to recognize the countryside: Volis. There were the hills of her hometown, once so beautiful, now a scab of what it once was. Her heart fell at the sight. There in the distance lay her father's stronghold, the fort, all now in ruins. It was a great heap of rubble, scattered with untended corpses sprawled in unnatural positions, visible even from here, looking up at the sky as if to ask Kyra how she could have let this happen to them.

Kyra shut her eyes and tried to push the image from her mind—yet she could not. It was too hard to just fly over this place that had once meant so much to her. She looked up toward the horizon, toward Marda, and she knew she should continue on, but something inside her could not bring herself to just pass over her hometown. She had to stop and see it for herself before she left Escalon, on what might be her final journey.

Kyra directed Theon to dive down, and she could feel him resisting—as if he, too, felt driven to stick with their mission and head to Marda. Reluctantly, though, he gave in.

They dove and landed in the center of what was once Volis, once a bustling stronghold filled with life—children, dance, song, smells of food, her father's proud warriors strutting to and fro. Kyra's breath caught as she dismounted and walked. She let out an involuntary cry. There was nothing here now. Just rubble and oppressive silence, broken only by the sound of Theon's heavy breathing, of his scraping the ground with his talons, as if he himself were enraged, as if eager to leave. She could not blame him: this town was now a tomb.

Gravel crunched beneath Kyra's boots as she slowly walked through the place, a gust of wind ripping through from the scorched plains surrounding the fort. She looked everywhere, needing to see, yet also needing to look away: it was like a nightmare. There was Shopkeepers Row, now nothing but a long pile of charred rubble; on her other side was the armory, now completely destroyed, a heap of stone, its front gate caved in. Before her, the great, towering fort, where her father had held so many feasts, where she herself had lived, now lay as a ruin, but a few walls left standing. Its gate was open, gaping, as if inviting the world to enter and see what it had once been.

As she walked, her heart pounding in her chest, Kyra knew she needed to see this, needed to see what become of her people in order to feel a sense of resolution. As much as she didn't want to, Kyra forced herself to look, to take it all in. She saw bodies of women and children, all lying dead in the streets, bodies twisted in unnatural positions. She saw a dozen of her father's men, Vidar in their center, all lying dead, face first by the castle's gate. She could see from the way they held their swords that they had all put up a fight, made a stand here. She shook her head in admiration: these brave men had fought fearlessly, despite the odds, facing off against an army.

Her eyes watered at the sight. They were an inspiration to her. They died for the revolution that *she* had sparked, and as she looked at them, she resolved that their deaths not be in vain.

Kyra's heart broke as she continued to walk, the signs of death all around her. What monsters could have done this? She looked closely and saw the huge claw marks on the bodies, and she knew this to be a troll attack. It was a sneak glimpse of what awaited her on the other side of the Flames.

Kyra slowly made her way toward her old fort. She passed through the destroyed doorway and entered the remnants of the building, eager to see this place she had once inhabited, this place she had been so sure would never fall.

It was cool in here, swirling with dust, unnaturally damp, as if spirits hung in the air. It felt conspicuously abandoned, felt as if she were visiting some distorted version of her past. It was as if her childhood memories had been destroyed and replaced.

Kyra passed what remained of a gaping stairway, now shattered in half, unable to ascend. She continued walking, straight ahead, in a daze, and entered what remained of her father's Great Hall, now nothing more than a pile of rubble. She passed behind a crack in the stone wall and found the entrance, still hidden, to her father's Chamber of Heroes.

Kyra entered and as she did, she stood there, numb. This small, hidden chamber, to her great relief, had been preserved. It was here where she had spent so many of her childhood days, dreaming, yearning, craving to be a warrior. There, to her relief, were the sculptures of the great warriors, still standing, the ones that had spurred her imagination as a child, had spurred her to want to achieve greatness. Sunlight poured in through gaps in the walls, high up, shining down on the sarcophagi of her ancestors. The outlines of their bodies lay face up in the stone, facing up proudly to the sky, staring into the heavens, eyes wide, as if even death held no fear for them. They were supposed to reside here for thousands of years. This room was supposed to stand the test of time.

"A powerful thing, to face our own mortality."

Kyra spun, raising her staff, tense, ready for battle, shocked that someone else was alive here, in the room with her.

But she relaxed when she recognized who it was. Softis the Wise. Volis's historian.

It felt so good to see an old face. There he stood, but feet away, looking older than ever. He had always looked old, but now he looked ancient. He stood hunched over in his robe, leaning on his staff, looking, if possible, even older than when she had left him.

"Softis."

She rushed forward, embracing him, and he hugged her back with his weak grip. It was like having a piece of her childhood restored to her once again.

"You survived," she said with a rush of relief, wiping away tears with the back of her hand.

He nodded, smiling weakly.

"My fate," he replied, his voice ancient and raspy, "my blessing and my curse. To survive life at every turn. Long after everyone I have known and loved is dead."

He sighed.

"They killed them all," he continued, shaking his head, looking to the floor with sadness. "Women and children, young and old, strong and lame. They killed all that remained of this fort."

"Trolls?" she asked warily, almost afraid to ask.

He nodded back solemnly.

"Your father could not have anticipated this," he replied. "Now all that we have left, ironically, are these tombs."

Softis stepped forward, limping through the room, running his hand along the bronze sculptures, along the stone sarcophagi.

"Great men they were," he said. "Men to look up to. Men whose problems were as pressing in their times as ours. They were men of valor. Men we must remember always."

He turned to her, his eyes aglow.

"They are *your* people, Kyra. Your blood. It runs through you, this blood of valor. Armis the Great: a man who killed a dozen men with a single pull of a bow. Arcard the Strong: a man who fought off a legion of soldiers with a single sword. Aseries the Lone: a man who fought alone, refused to stand with an army, and killed more men on his own than entire villages together."

He turned to her.

"These are *you*, Kyra. You are not separate from them. You are one and the same. Your ancestors' blood courses through you, and they all watch over you. They all depend on you now. You are all they have left."

He stepped forward and grasped her shoulders with a surprising strength.

"Don't you see, Kyra? You are all they have left."

He stared into her eyes, a glimmer of his old intensity shining through, like a candle on its last flame.

"What will you do, Kyra? Will you make them proud?"

She nodded back gravely.

"Yes," she said, meaning it. "I will."

"Even if it means risking your life?"

"Yes," she replied. "With all that I am."

42

She felt her words were true, and as she spoke them, she felt a vibration run through her palms, as if the spirits lingering in the room had heard her and had approved.

Softis stared at her for a long time, as if gauging the truth of what she said, and finally he nodded in approval.

"Good," he said.

He sighed and withdrew his hand, yet still he studied her.

"Of all the great men," he added, "who had ever fought for Volis, of all the warriors they thought would be the standard bearer, the greatest of them all was *you*, Kyra."

Kyra stared back, shocked.

"Me?" she asked.

He nodded.

"That was what they could not have seen," he replied. "All along, for all these generations, it was *you* they were waiting for. *You*, a simple girl, who is far more than that."

Kyra's hands trembled as she pondered the weight of his words.

"Do not shy from danger, Kyra," he urged. "Seek it out. That is the only way to save your life."

CHAPTER ELEVEN

Kyle opened his eyes, disoriented, wondering where he was. He reached out and felt cold grass and dirt between his fingers, felt a heavy weight atop him, nearly suffocating him. He also felt something curious licking his palm, nudging him awake.

Kyle leaned back and shoved off the armor. Breathing hard from the effort, free of the weight, Kyle looked about and was horrified at what he saw. He was surrounded by dead bodies. He lay in a field of corpses—thousands of them—Pandesian soldiers and trolls mingled together, all charred, faces frozen in death masks of agony. The land, too, was scorched around them, burned by the dragons' breath, and as Kyle pushed the last of the shields and heavy armor off of him, he realized at once that the only reason he had survived was because of the metal and corpses shielding him.

He continued to feel the tongue on his palm, and Kyle, remembering, looked over and was shocked at who he saw: Leo. Kyra's wolf. Somehow it had sought him out, had found him, had crossed Escalon searching for him, and had nudged him awake. Of course, it made sense: Leo was fanatically devoted to Kyra, and he must have sensed that Kyle could lead him to her. That also, though, meant something else: Kyra and Leo had gotten separated. Kyle's heart fell, as he wondered what may have happened to her.

Kyle heard a snort, a clawing at the grass, and he turned to see Kyra's horse, Andor, standing nearby, waiting impatiently, too. Kyle marveled at the loyalty of her animals.

Kyle rubbed Leo's head as he sat up, his head aching, wondering how much time had passed. He was singed, aching, scratched and wounded on nearly every part of his body. Yet he was alive. He was the lone man here, in this battlefield of the dead, now a massive cemetery.

There came a distant rumble, and Kyle looked up, bracing himself as he examined the sky. On the horizon he spotted the faint remnants of the flock of dragons, flying away, presumably south, for Andros. They must have assumed everyone was dead.

Kyle stood, knowing he was lucky to be alive, shocked the dragons had reached Escalon. He closed his eyes, as he did when summoning his powers, and tried to use them to show him where to go, what his purpose was now. Kyra was somewhere, he did not know where, far away, Escalon was in ruin, and the Tower of Ur was destroyed. What purpose did life hold for him?

Kyle closed his eyes and focused, and as he did, a driving sense of purpose came to him. It commanded him to look up, to search the skies. Kyle did so, and he suddenly saw something fly overhead, just a flash, racing by, in and out of the clouds. A dragon. Yet it flew in the opposite direction of the flock. It was unlike the others. It was a baby. And it flew alone.

And on its back, Kyle felt a chill to realize, was someone he knew. Someone he loved.

Kyra.

Kyle was overcome as he watched the dragon disappear on the horizon. Kyra was flying north. But where? Why? At least that explained why she and Leo and Andor became separated.

Kyle closed his eyes and tuned in, summoning his powers, wondering. None of it seemed to make any sense.

And then it came to him.

Marda.

A chill ran up his arms as he saw Kyra's future. He saw her enveloped by blackness, saw the evil awaiting her, the death surrounding her. He saw, most of all, that she would never return.

Flooded by a new sense of purpose, Kyle broke into a sprint, running north through the fields, faster and faster. Leo and Andor ran by his side, joining him, yet he was even faster than they. He was as fast as a bird, as fast as a dragon, covering so much ground so fast, that soon, he would reach the Flames. He would enter the land of Marda, do whatever it took to find and saved the girl he loved.

Wait, Kyra, he urged. *Wait for me.*

CHAPTER TWELVE

Aidan stood in the cave amongst all his father's soldiers, his father in the center, hundreds of men crowding him in a semicircle, all intently looking at their commander with love and respect—and Aidan felt a rush of pride. Beside him stood Anvin and Motley and Cassandra, White at his feet, and Aidan was elated to be here, to be included amongst all these great men, and most of all, to be reunited with his father again. No matter what should happen, for now at least, all was right in the world again.

It was a jubilant scene, all these warriors clearly happy to be reunited, all embracing and talking, discussing their predicament as they had for hours, ever since Kyra had dropped them here in this remote cave. They all knew the situation was dire. They needed an urgent plan, and they debated a course of action heatedly, all professional warriors, all with varying opinions. His father stood in the middle of it all, listening, judging, weighing their opinions.

"We must return and storm the capital!" Bramthos exclaimed to a group of men. "We must attack while they are distracted, while the dragons attack them. We can exploit their weakness."

"And what of the dragons?" Kavos called out. "Shall they not kill us, too?"

"We can attack them fast, and then take shelter," Bramthos countered.

The others shook their heads.

"Reckless," Seavig replied. "More of us will die by the dragons' breath than by the Pandesians' sword."

"Then what would you have us do? Remain here, hiding in this cave?" Arthfael countered.

Kavos shook his head.

"No," Kavos replied. "Yet we cannot return to Andros. Nor can we risk confronting them head on."

"The Pandesians must be attacked," Bramthos insisted. "If we wait for them to pursue us—and pursue us they shall—then we shall be attacked on their terms. Andros now sits in disarray, yet soon those dragons will retreat. Shall we then confront a million men in the open field?"

46

"Who's to say the dragons will retreat?" Seavig argued. "Maybe they will burn Andros until there is nothing left."

"Why have they come to begin with?" called out another.

The cave broke into heated debate, men talking over each other, arguing, none agreeing and all agitated.

Duncan stood in the midst of it all, his fist on his chin, deep in thought. Aidan could tell from the familiar look on his face that he was agitated, mulling it all over. He rubbed his beard, and Aidan knew that to be a sign he was coming close to a decision.

Suddenly, Anvin stepped forward.

"Duncan is our commander," he yelled above the din of the crowd. "He has always led us brilliantly. I defer to his opinion."

The rowdy group of men finally fell silent as all eyes turned to Duncan.

Duncan sighed. He slowly stepped forward, stood to his full height, and addressed the group of warriors.

"First, I cannot express to you my gratitude," he said, his deep, authoritative voice echoing off the walls. "You returned to Andros for me. You saved my life, against every chance. I owe you my life."

They all looked back at him with respect and appreciation.

"I had made a foolish decision," Duncan continued, "to trust them, to negotiate, and it is a mistake I shall not make again."

"We will follow you anywhere, Duncan," Seavig called out, while the others cheered.

"Just tell us where to go next," Arthfael called. "Shall we return to the capital?"

Aidan felt his heart pounding as the silence thickened and he wondered what his father might say.

"No," Duncan finally said.

His single word was filled with such confidence, it left no room for another choice.

"We would catch them off guard, true," he said. "Yet we would lose too many of us. And we would be fighting in *their* territory, against their defenses, and on their terms. The chaos would serve us, but it could also work against us."

He rubbed his beard.

"No," he added. "We shall lead them to us."

They all stared back, looking surprised.

"Bring them here?" Bramthos asked.

Duncan shook his head.

"No," he replied. "We shall lure them to a place where we will have the advantage, where they will be sure to lose. A place that takes advantage of our knowledge of our homeland. A place where we own the land."

"And where is that, my commander?" Arthfael asked.

Duncan drew his sword, the sound echoing off the walls. He stepped forward, reached out, and slowly etched a long line in the sand. At its end, he drew a circle, and he pointed the sword's tip right in the center.

They all crowded around, close.

Duncan looked up and met their eyes with deadly seriousness.

"Baris," he finally said.

Silence fell over the room as the men closed in and craned their necks.

"Baris?" Bramthos asked, surprised. "Lure them to a canyon? That would give us the low ground."

"It is also hostile ground," Seavig added. "Teeming with Baris's men."

Duncan grinned for the first time.

"Exactly," he replied.

The group fell silent, clearly baffled. Anvin, though, nodded.

"I see what you see," Anvin said. "Vengeance against Baris— and at the same time, a chance to kill the Pandesians."

Duncan nodded back.

"Bant will not anticipate our attack," Duncan replied.

"But why kill our countrymen first when we must face the Pandesian army?" Bramthos called out.

"We must first and foremost kill those men who betrayed us, who betrayed their homeland," Duncan replied. "Who lay at our flank. Otherwise, we will never be safe. Then, with Bant's men dead, we can lure the Pandesians to us."

"Yet they will have the high ground," Seavig said.

"Which is why we will lure them down, inside the canyon," Duncan replied.

They all seemed baffled.

"And then what?" Bramthos asked.

Duncan looked back, cold and hard.

48

"Flood it," Duncan replied.

They all stared back in shock.

"Flood it?" Seavig finally asked. "How?"

Duncan raised his sword and continued drawing his line in the sand, until finally he drew three short marks.

"Everfall," he stated. "We will redirect the falls. Its waters will flow north, and flood the canyon."

He stared at the men, who looked down, shocked.

"A few hundred of us cannot kill Pandesia's thousands," he replied. "Yet nature can."

A long silence fell over the men as they looked at Duncan, all rubbing their beards, all deep in thought.

"Risky," Kavos finally said. "It is a long stretch between here and Baris. Anything could happen."

"And the canyon has never been flooded before," Seavig added. "What if it doesn't work?"

"And if we lose against Baris?" Bramthos asked. "That itself could be a deadly battle."

"Not to mention, Leptus controls the falls," Anvin added. "We'd need to enlist their help if we stand any chance."

Duncan nodded to him.

"Precisely, my friend," he replied. "And that is why I am dispatching you at once."

Anvin's eyes widened as he looked back with surprise and pride.

"Leave at once for Leptus," Duncan added, "and enlist them in our plan."

A long silence filled the air, the men on the fence, until finally Kavos stepped forward. All the others looked at him with respect, and Aidan knew that whatever he said would mean their agreement or not.

"A daring plan," Kavos said. "A risky plan, a bold plan. A plan that will most likely fail. Yet one which is valorous. And foolhardy. I like it. I am with Duncan."

One at a time all the men looked up and shouted in agreement, raising their swords.

"I AM WITH DUNCAN!" they all cried out.

And Aidan's heart soared with pride.

*

Aidan walked beside Duncan, his father's strong hand on his shoulder, their boots crunching gravel as they crossed the cave, past all the warriors donning armor, sharpening swords, preparing for their next battle. Aidan had never felt more proud than at this moment. His father, owning the respect of all the men in this cave after his stirring speech, had come not to join his commanders, but to Aidan, all eyes on them. He had pulled Aidan aside and walked with him, alone. As all the men watched them, Aidan took it as a great sign of respect; he hadn't even realized his father was aware of him amongst all these men, let alone at this critical time.

They walked in silence, Aidan waiting, eager to hear what his father had to say.

"I never forget," his father said, as they finally crossed out of earshot of the other men. He stopped and looked at Aidan meaningfully, and Aidan stared back, his heart pounding. "I know what you did back there. You came for me, all the way from Volis. You trekked alone, all the way to the capital, a dangerous journey even for a hard warrior. You survived, and you even managed to find men to help you."

His father grinned, and Aidan, welling with pride, smiled back.

"You managed to make your way into the dungeons," his father continued, "in a city occupied, and to help free me in my bleakest hour. If it weren't for you, I would still be chained there—if not already at the executioner's hand. I owe you my life, son," he said, and Aidan felt his eyes well. "You have proved on this day that you are not only a valued son, but a fine, budding warrior. One day you will take over my command."

Aidan's eyes lit up at his father's words. It was the first time his father had ever talked to him this way, with this tone, looked at him with such respect. They were words he'd always longed to hear from his father, words that made everything in the world right, that made everything he had suffered worth it.

"There was nothing else I could even think of doing," Aidan replied. "I love you, Father. There has never been anything else I've wanted to do but help your cause."

Duncan nodded back, and this time his eyes welled with tears.

"I know that, son."

50

Aidan felt his heart pounding as he summoned the courage to make a request.

"I wish to accompany Aidan on his trip to Leptus."

Duncan stared back, eyes widening in surprise.

"I wish to be of service, *real* service," Aidan continued in a rush, "and I long to take the journey. I will be of little service here, with all your warriors, attacking the canyon. But I can be of great service in helping Anvin make his way across the countryside, reach Leptus, and persuade them to join our cause. Please, Father. It would be a noble mission."

Duncan stroked his beard, seemingly lost in thought. But then, to Aidan's disappointment, he finally shook his head.

"The journey to Leptus is a long and treacherous one," he said, his voice heavy. "One even Anvin may not survive. Aside from the hostile landscape, dragons still circle and packs of Pandesian soldiers roam. You may even face a hostile reception in Leptus—they are separatists, don't forget."

Aidan did not hesitate.

"I know all this, Father. And none of that deters me."

His father slowly shook his head, as he fell silent, a stubborn look that Aidan knew meant No. Aidan summoned more resolve.

"Did you not just say I have proven myself?" Aidan pressed. "I have crossed Escalon alone for you. Let me cross the wasteland. Let me show you your faith in me is not misplaced. I *need* this, Father. I need my own mission. I need to feel like I, too, am a man. And I shall never be a man hiding here under your wings."

Duncan stared back for a long time, and Aidan could see the thoughts turning in his head, as his heart pounded, awaiting the response.

Finally, his father sighed, reached out and squeezed his shoulder.

"You are an even braver warrior than I thought," he said, "and a more loyal son. You are right—I have underestimated you. And it is not for a father to hold back a son hoping to become a man."

He grinned and nodded.

"Go with Anvin. Serve our cause and serve it well."

Aidan beamed as his heart filled with pride and gratitude.

A group of soldiers appeared and interrupted, leading Duncan away on other business, while at the same time, Motley came over to Aidan's side, along with Cassandra and White.

Aidan saw Motley looking down at him with concern.

"Do you really think that wise?" Motley asked.

Aidan looked at him with surprise.

"Were you eavesdropping?" Aidan asked.

Motley grinned.

"I'm an actor. Eavesdropping is my trade. Keep no secrets from me, boy. Not after what we've been through."

Aidan sighed, realizing Motley was who he was.

"Yes," he admitted. "I am going. And yes, it was wise."

White barked at his feet and jumped up and licked his palm, and Aidan laughed.

"I guess you want to come, too."

White wagged his tail wildly, clearly answering him, and Aidan liked the idea of having the companionship.

"A foolish errand, boy," Motley scoffed. "You may not survive it. What is it with you and valor? Have you not yet learned your lesson?"

Aidan smiled, undeterred.

"I have not even *begun* to learn my lesson," he replied. "And why should it concern you?"

"Why should it concern me?" Motley asked, offended. "I risked my hide a dozen times to keep you alive. Does that mean nothing? Do you think I wish to see you dead? I care for you, boy. God knows why—I shouldn't—but I do. Maybe it's your foolish recklessness. Maybe it's your naivete, your optimism. In any case, stop this. Go tell your father you made a mistake and stay here with me and the rest of the men. There's safety in numbers. You will die out there alone."

Aidan shook his head.

"You just don't understand me," he said. "That is not who I am. There is more danger in trying to save your life than in being willing to lose it."

Motley scoffed.

"That sounds like something from one of those old books of yours. I told you to stop reading about the past. Those warriors are all dead now. Where did all their valor get them?"

Aidan frowned.

"Their valor made their lives worth living, and it is the only reason we even remember their names today," Aidan replied.

"And what then is so great about being remembered?" Motley countered. "Will you really even care if you are remembered once you are dead?"

Aidan went to respond, but Motley raised a hand.

"I see there's no sense that can be talked into you, boy," Motley added. "But I will tell you there is a danger in being a warrior before your time. It is not yet your time."

"Then when is my time?" Aidan rebuffed angrily. "When I'm old and gray? Your time comes when it chooses you—not when you choose it."

Motley sighed long and hard.

"I was afraid you'd say something like that. Something bold and foolish. Very well, then. Since there's no changing your mind, at least take this."

Aidan looked down and was surprised as Motley reached out and placed something in his hand. He examined it, baffled, turning it over in his palm. It looked like a piece of curved ivory.

"What is it?" Aidan asked.

Motley reached out and grabbed the two ends of the ivory and separated them, and to Aidan's shock, a concealed blade appeared, gleaming.

"A dagger," Aidan breathed, in awe.

Motley nodded with pride.

"As sharp as you'll find in the kingdom, and as well hidden."

He reached up and clasped Aidan's shoulder.

"Just be sure to return it to me. I don't like to see my weapons lost. Especially stage weapons. They're hard to come by, you know."

Aidan's eyes welled with gratitude as he realized Motley's concern for him. He stepped forward and hugged Motley, and Motley hugged him back.

Motley then stepped back.

"I never had a son, you know," he said to Aidan, looking down with pride and sadness.

Then, quickly, before Aidan could respond, he turned and walked away.

53

Aidan watched him go, filled with gratitude, seeing what a great friend Motley had become. He had been wrong, he realized, to have judged him and dismissed him merely because he was an actor and not a warrior. Motley was, in his own way, a finer warrior than many of the others here, Aidan realized. He had his own sense of valor.

Aidan heard a shuffling of feet, and he turned to see Cassandra standing close by, waiting for him. As she looked at him, he saw something in her eyes he had not seen before. Something like caring.

"So you are just going to leave me alone with all these men, are you?" she asked.

Aidan smiled, feeling a wave of guilt at leaving her.

"My father will care for you like a daughter," he replied.

She shook her head and there flashed in her eyes a glimpse of the defiance, the steel-like resolve, that had kept her alive on the streets.

"I don't need taking care of," she replied proudly. "I've taken care of myself all my life. What I want is to join you."

Aidan stared back, surprised. He wondered if she wanted to go on the journey, or if she wanted to be with him.

"It is no journey for you," he answered.

"And yet it is for you?" she asked.

He frowned.

"What if you came and something happened to you?" he asked. "It would be on my head."

"It is on your head anyway," she answered with a smile. "You saved me. I would be dead otherwise. So anything that happens to me from now on is on your head."

Aidan shook his head sadly.

"I will come back for you," he said solemnly. "I promise."

He reached out a hand, and as she slowly placed hers in his, he felt a thrill at the warmth of her touch. It made him feel alive, alive in a way he never had before.

She began to pull her hand away, and as she did, Aidan found himself leaning in. His heart pounded and, not even fully aware of what he was doing, he placed his lips, so gently, on hers.

He kissed her, and as he did, he felt more terrified than he had of any foe, of any battle. What if she rejected him?

Slowly, Cassandra leaned back and stared at him, wide-eyed, seeming stunned.

She frowned.

"Why did you do that?" she demanded, sounding upset.

Aidan gulped, worried that he had offended her, that he had misread the situation, that she did not care for him that way after all.

"I'm sorry…" he mumbled. "I…didn't mean…to offend you."

He stood there, feeling a cold sweat rise up, when suddenly she surprised him by smiling wide.

"Whatever it was," she replied, "come back soon. And do it again."

CHAPTER THIRTEEN

The Supreme and Holy Ra fell from his balcony, tumbling through the air after the dragon had sliced the stone, flailing down toward the stone courtyard far below. He felt his life flashing before his eyes, saw all his conquests, his triumphs, his victories—and realized that he was not yet ready to die. He was, he knew, greater than death. He was The One Who Could Not Die, and as he fell, he became enraged with Death, determined to vanquish him, determined, at all costs, *not* to die.

Ra looked down as he fell and saw his soldiers, many on fire, shrieking, running in a panic through the streets as they tried to get away from the dragons' flame. It was a scene of devastation. But even in the devastation, Ra knew, there was hope. There was always, he knew, a way out.

Ra set his sights on a group of his men, directly below him, and he twisted and contorted his body in the air, aiming to fall right for them. It was a good fall, thirty feet through the air, and he aimed for the top of their heads. He knew that landing on them would crush their skulls, would drive them into the ground. But it would also, he knew, mean a cushion for a soft landing for him. It would be an honor for them, he decided, to die in his service.

As Ra neared the ground, he suddenly felt his feet impacting their heads, felt his entire body landing atop them, crushing them. He could hear their bones break beneath him as they cushioned his fall.

Ra landed, tumbling to the ground, winded. Yet as he rolled to his feet, he knew, with great relief, that he was alive, and that nothing was broken. He looked over to see his men beside him, with broken necks, not so lucky.

Ra grinned. He felt victorious. He had cheated death.

Filled with fury at the dragons, which Ra considered a mere nuisance, he strutted through the streets, bent on vengeance. What bothered him most was not the dragons, but that Duncan, his great prize, had escaped. Whatever the cost, he had to get him back.

A great dragon roared, and Ra looked up to see him diving down straight for him, opening his mouth and breathing fire. Ra, fearless, quickly grabbed several of his men and threw them across the courtyard, distracting the dragon. The dragon turned to them, and Ra used the opportunity to duck behind a stone wall. As the dragon breathed down, its flames incinerated his men but licked past Ra, protected by the stone.

Ra stood there, his back up against the wall, and as he saw more and more dragons diving down, he knew he had to do something quickly. All around him scores of his men, aflame, shrieked and fell, collapsing to their deaths. He was fast losing his army.

A group of generals spotted him and ran to his side, cowering around him, taking shelter behind the stone and awaiting his command. All eyes on him, Ra scanned the courtyard, momentarily blinded by the sunlight reflecting off the huge golden shields dropped by his men—and an idea came to him.

"Those shields!" he commanded.

Ra suddenly ran out into the open courtyard, fearlessly leading the pack, and his men followed as he went for the shields. Ra picked one up himself, huge, heavy, and his dozens of men followed his lead, lining up beside him.

"Crouch!" Ra commanded.

He dropped to his knees and held his shield overhead. The others followed, and soon there was a wall of metal pointing up at the sky.

Another wave of flames came down, and this time they rolled off the shields and harmlessly continued on their way. Ra felt the tremendous heat on the other side of the shield, nearly scorching the back of his hand as he held on. It felt as if it would burn right through, yet he held on tight.

"HOLD!" he commanded his men.

Most listened, but a few, clearly afraid, let go and ran. As they did, they were burned alive.

Finally, the wave of flames passed, and Ra breathed hard, sweating, elated he was alive.

"TURN THE SHIELDS!" he commanded.

Ra's men did as he commanded, turning the shields, as did he, until they caught the angle of the sun. They finally caught the rays, and as they did, it reflected a blinding column of sunlight back up into the sky.

The dragons, diving down, suddenly recoiled, clearly unable to see. They stopped in mid-air and swatted at the light with their talons, as if trying to block it out, trying to see again.

It was just what he needed. He had stunned the dragons long enough to mobilize his men and escape from the city. Before he did, though, he knew he had just one more thing to do.

"General!" he commanded, turning to one of his long-trusted advisors, a man who had served with him across the world. "Lead your battalion of men north, out in the open courtyard and through the northern gates of the city."

The general stared back in fear and shock.

"But my Most Holy Ra," he began, tremulous, "that would leave my men exposed. We would die."

Ra nodded.

"True," he replied. "Yet you will die here if you defy my command."

Ra nodded to the others, and they all drew swords and pointed them at the general.

The general, panic-stricken, jumped to his feet and shouted orders to his men. Ra watched as he led them, hundreds of men, marching out in the open square and toward the northern gate of the city.

"The rest of you, follow me!" Ra cried.

He turned and ran, and his thousands of other men followed him for the southern end of Andros, as horns were sounded up and down the city. High above, the dragons began to roar as the shields were lowered and they were no longer blinded.

As he ran south, Ra glanced back over his shoulder and watched as the dragons, as he had hoped, fixed their sights on his exposed general, heading north, alone, with his men. Ra smiled as the dragons dove down for his decoy. They breathed fire, and his general shrieked, aflame, as he and all his men ran for the gates, aflame.

Ra turned back to the Southern Gate, running to freedom. The general and his division were a small price to pay for his own safety.

They finally all passed through the Southern Gate, and as they did, Ra breathed easy as he saw the open stretch of barren land before him. The south lay before him, where, he knew, Duncan had fled.

Ra mounted the horse with the golden harness that was quickly led to him.

"ADVANCE!" he commanded.

There came a thunderous roar as thousands of Pandesian soldiers mounted horses and followed him, racing south across the barren wasteland, somewhere toward Duncan. This time, Ra would not let him out of his grasp.

CHAPTER FOURTEEN

Alec stood at the bow of the ship as they sailed out of the Lost Isles, navigating around the strange outcroppings of barren rock, the seagrass making a strange noise as it brushed up against the hull. The water was as still as could be, eerily calm. Mist rose off it, casting a magical light, and it all felt surreal to him as he sailed at the head of a fleet. Behind him, all the men of the Lost Isles followed him as he sailed out into the Sea of Tears.

Alec felt the humming in his hand, and he looked down, awestruck, at the magnificent weapon he was holding. The Unfinished Sword. It felt surreal to be holding it. He raised it up to the light, barely paying attention to the water all around him, fixated only by this magnificent piece of metal. He twisted and turned it as he held it high, the light reflecting off it in a magical way, and he felt it was greater than him. Greater than all of them.

Alec marveled at it. It was the greatest weapon he had ever held, the only weapon he had ever wielded that he did not fully understand, that felt bigger than he. It was a weapon of such extraordinary beauty, extraordinary magic, that he hardly even knew what to make of it. He knew he had helped forge it, yet a part of felt him that it wasn't his creation at all. He squeezed the hilt, interlaced with rubies and diamonds, studied the strange inscriptions on its blade, ancient, mysterious, and knew its origins lay somewhere in history, thousands of years ago. He could only wonder who had begun this weapon—and why it had been unfinished. Had Sovos' words been true? Did Alex really have a special destiny?

Alec glanced back over his shoulder, saw his large wooden ship filled with hundreds of islanders, as were all the other ships in the fleet, and he felt the pressure on him. Where exactly were they all heading? Why did they need him? What would his role would be in all this? He did not fully understand it, but he sensed that, for the first time in his life, he was caught up in a destiny bigger than himself.

"They have never left the isles before, you know," came a voice.

Alec turned to see Sovos standing beside him, looking down at him with a serious expression, dressed in his aristocratic outfit. He remained as mysterious to Alec as he had been on the day they had met in Ur.

Alec was surprised to hear that.

"Never?" he asked, turning and surveying the warriors of the Lost Isles.

Sovos shook his head.

"They've never had cause to leave. Not until this day. Not until you finished forging the sword."

Alec felt the weight of responsibility.

"I don't feel like I finished it," he replied. "Something just came to me and I followed a hunch."

"It was more than a hunch," Sovos corrected. "Only *you* could forge it."

Alec felt frustrated.

"But I still don't understand how I did it."

"Sometimes we don't understand all that we do," Sovos replied. "Sometimes we are just the channel, and we must be grateful for that. Sometimes we harness forces greater than ourselves, forces that we shall never understand. We all have a role to play."

Sovos turned and looked out at the sea, and Alec studied it, too. The mist was beginning to burn off the water as they began to leave the archipelago of the Lost Isles and head out to sea. The waters were becoming rougher, too.

"Where are we sailing?" Alec asked. "Where are they bringing the sword?"

Sovos studied the sea.

"It is not them," he replied. "But *you*. You are leading them."

Alec looked back, shocked.

"Leading them? Me? I don't even know where we're going."

"To Escalon, of course."

Alec's eyes widened.

"Why? Escalon is overrun. The Pandesians inhabit it now. To sail back there would be to sail to our deaths!"

Sovos continued to study the sea, expressionless.

"It is far worse than you think," he said. "The dragons have arrived in Escalon, too."

61

Alec's eyes widened again.

"The dragons?" he asked, astounded.

"They've flown thousands of miles and crossed the great sea," Sovos continued. "And they have come for one special thing."

"What?" Alec asked.

But Sovos ignored his question.

The current picked up, and Alec felt a tightness in his chest as he thought about their sailing closer and closer to Escalon, to a land filled with dragons and inhabited by Pandesian soldiers.

"Why would we sail to our deaths?" he pressed.

Sovos finally turned to him.

"Because of what you hold in your hand," he replied. "It is all that Escalon has left now."

Alec looked down at the sword in his palm with an even greater sense of awe and wonder.

"You really think this small piece of metal will have any effect against Pandesia? Against a host of dragons?" he asked, dreading the journey before them. For the first time in his life, Alec felt certain that he was heading to his death.

"Sometimes, my dear boy," Sovos said, laying a hand on his shoulder, "a small piece of metal is the only hope there is."

CHAPTER FIFTEEN

Merk looked out at the Three Daggers as they sailed past them, craggy islands emerging from the bay, steep, vertical, and devoid of life. Covered in strange, angry black birds with large red eyes that cawed fiercely at them as they passed, the isles were covered in the mist of the bay, the relentless waves of the Bay of Death smashing up against them as if trying to knock them back into the sea. It sent up clouds of white foam and mist toward Merk's boat, dousing it, and he studied the scene in wonder. He was grateful he was not to be stranded here, the most desolate and unforgiving place he had ever seen. It made the Devil's Finger seem hospitable.

"The Three Daggers," came the voice.

Merk turned to see Lorna standing beside him, holding the rail, studying the sea with her large, glowing blue eyes, silvery-blonde hair. She stood there calmly, despite the violent currents of the Bay of Death, a beacon of life against the bleak landscape, staring out at the sea as if she and the waters were one.

"The isles said to be forged by the great goddess Inka. Legend tells she spewed forth her anger from the sea when looking for her three lost daughters," she added. "Beyond the third lies the isle of Knossos."

Merk looked out and saw, just beyond the third rocky isle, an isle of cliffs rising straight out of the sea, ringed by a narrow, rocky shore. At its top was a flat plateau, and atop this sat a fort built a hundred feet high. It was squat, square, gray, and adorned with ancient battlements; its walls had long, narrow slits cut in them, behind which Merk could see the tips of glistening arrows at the ready. The fort was a stout, ugly thing, as if one with the rock itself, sprayed by mist and wind and breaking waves, and taking it all in stride.

Even more impressive were the warriors that Merk spotted as they sailed closer. The wind and the currents carried them at full speed now, right for its shores, and soon Merk could see their hardened faces staring out. He could see even from here that they were the faces of surly men, men who had no joy in life. They lined the battlements like goats, hundreds of them, peering out into the sea as if eagerly awaiting an enemy.

They were the hardest-looking men Merk had ever seen—and that was saying a lot. They were donned in gray armor, with gray swords and gray helmets, the same color of the rock behind them, their visors pulled down, narrow slits for eyes looking out behind the helmets. These men looked as if they, too, had been forged from the rock. They were men who did not even budge when a gale of wind arrived that was strong enough to turn Merk's boat sideways. They looked as if they were rooted to the place, a part of the very earth itself.

Here, at last, was Knossos, the last outpost off the last peninsula of Escalon, right in the center of the swirling waters of the Bay of Death. It was the most remote place Merk had ever seen, and clearly not for the faint of heart.

"What is their purpose of this place?" Merk asked. "What do they defend?"

Lorna shook her head, still looking out.

"There are many things you have yet to understand," she replied. "We all have a role to play in the coming war."

As they neared, Merk found himself silently reaching under his shirt and gripping his dagger, though he knew it would do no good. It was an old habit he had, whenever he was nervous. He saw the long bows over these warriors' shoulders, saw the strange weapons they held in their hands—long, dangling chains with spikes at the end—and he knew he was vastly outnumbered. It made him feel vulnerable. It was a feeling he had rarely felt before—he had always made a point of planning ahead, of never putting himself in such a position.

The currents picked up and their ship soon touched the shore, a hard bump onto the craggy beach. Without pausing, Lorna jumped off and landed on the sand, walking gracefully, not missing a beat, while Merk fumbled to get off the edge of the ship as it rocked. He landed clumsily behind her, his boots splashing in the freezing waters as he tried to catch up.

He followed Lorna as she approached a group of waiting soldiers and stopped before one, apparently their commander, standing out front before the others, nearly twice Merk's size. The soldier looked graciously down at Lorna but then looked over at Merk and scowled down at him as if he were intruding. Merk tightened his grip on his dagger.

The soldier turned back to Lorna and half-bowed.

"My lady," he said deferentially.

"Thurn," she replied. Are my Watchers safe?" she asked.

He nodded back.

"Every one of them," he replied. He turned to Merk. "And who is this beside you?" he asked, tightening his grip on his chain.

"A friend," she replied. "He's not to be harmed."

The soldier reluctantly tore his gaze from Merk and looked back at her. Merk did not like being on this isle, but he did like hearing the word *friend*. He'd never had anyone call him a friend before, and for some reason, it touched him. The more he thought about it, the more he realized he felt a strong connection to Lorna, too. He wondered if she were just using the term, or if she genuinely felt the same way about him.

"An army of trolls follows on our heels," she said, in a rush. "We cannot defend. Not even you. Come with us to the mainland. We shall continue the battle in Escalon."

The soldier stared back at her solemnly.

"We are of Knossos," he replied. "We retreat from no enemy."

"Even if death is certain?" she pressed.

"*Especially* if death is certain," he replied. "To run would be to lose our honor—and honor is more sacred than life. Take your Watchers and go to the mainland. We shall make our stand here."

Lorna sighed, clearly frustrated.

"You would be killed here for harboring my people. I cannot allow that."

"We would be killed for doing our duty," he replied.

Lorna frowned, realizing she was getting nowhere.

"Don't you understand?" she added. "You face monsters. Not humans. Trolls—honorless, nasty creatures. They have no regard for life. They are crossing the Bay of Death and will soon surround this fort. Now is your chance to escape. Leave, and live to fight another day, in another place, on your terms. There are other ways to win. To stay here means death."

For the first time, the soldier grinned, as he looked out and scanned the horizon behind her.

"An honorable death, encircled by my foes," he replied, "is all I have ever prayed for. All that my men have ever prayed for. The gods have answered our prayers on this day."

Behind him, all the warriors of Knossos, all lined up with perfect discipline, suddenly raised their chains high in the air and grunted in agreement. They all stared back through the metal slats of their helmets, fearless.

Merk had never seen such a display of courage, and he was moved by it. For the first time in his life, he felt as if here, on this isle, with these men, he was part of something greater, of the cause he had so desperately sought.

Lorna turned to Merk, looking resigned.

"Go," she said. "Sail our ship to the mainland. Go to Leptus. You will be safe there. You can make your way to the capital and fight for our cause."

Merk was filled with admiration for her as he realized she meant to stay here.

He slowly shook his head, having already come to his own conclusion. Instead, he turned to Thurn and smiled.

"You intend to fight to the death, do you not?" he asked.

Thurn nodded back.

"I do," he replied.

Merk grinned.

"How heavy are those chains?" he asked.

Thurn looked down, seemingly surprised at the question, then finally, realizing that Merk meant to stay, he stared back approvingly. He nodded, and a soldier rushed forward and handed Merk an extra chain and spike.

Merk tested the weight of it; it was heavier than he thought. He swung it around and was amazed to see the iron spike at the end swing overhead like lightning. It made a high-pitched whistling noise as it swung. It was an unusual and substantial weapon, and he was impressed.

"Want one more man?" he asked.

For the first time, Thurn grinned back at Merk.

"I suppose," he replied, "we can always make room."

CHAPTER SIXTEEN

Kyra held tight to Theon's scales as they flew north, racing through the clouds, the sky around them darkening into a gloom as they neared the land of Marda. Softis's words still rang in her head as she recalled her eerie visit to Volis, her visit with her ancestors, their spirits lingering as if they were still with her.

Do not shy from danger, Kyra. Seek it out. That is the only way to save your life.

She felt it to be true. She felt she was on a sacred mission, and she felt the responsibility of living up to her bloodline, of all her ancestors, of achieving what they could not. True freedom for Escalon. Safety from the trolls. Safety from the dragons. Why was it, she wondered, that true freedom was always so elusive? That true safety was always so hard to achieve, generation after generation?

Flying further and further north, Kyra felt an increasing chill in the air. It was not so much the cold and the gloom as it was a sense of impending evil. She looked down, hoping to catch one last glimpse of Escalon before entering Marda, and expecting to see what she saw every day of her life growing up in Volis: the massive Wall of Flames shooting up into the sky, lighting the oncoming night. It would be thrilling to fly over them, to see how high they rose.

And yet, as she flew closer to the border and peered down below, she was baffled to see nothing. She looked twice, unsure of herself.

"Lower, Theon," she commanded.

Theon dove lower, descending through layer after layer of thick, black clouds, until finally they burst through and she caught a glimpse of the landscape below.

Her heart stopped in her chest.

There, below her, was a sight which would be forever ingrained in her soul. A sight which made her lose all hope. Kyra was shocked not by what she saw—but by what she did *not* see. By the *absence*. There, below, the Flames were gone.

For the first time in her life, Kyra saw the northern border not dominated by their ever-present glow, their crackle. What stood instead was charred land and open sky, with no barrier left between

Escalon and Marda. The sacred wall of protection, the magical Flames, forever guarded by her forefathers, stood no more.

Even more shocking, in its place Kyra saw the nation of trolls racing across the landscape, flooding her homeland, the two countries now one, with nothing to stop them. Thousands upon thousands of trolls raced by underneath her, like a heard of buffalo, their rumble and cheering audible even from here. They were leaving Marda by the millions, a great migration, and invading her country.

Kyra's blood boiled at the sight. She could already see all the burned, ransacked villages left in their wake, could already see the destruction this tidal wave of trolls was bringing to her homeland.

"Theon, down!" she yelled.

Theon needed no prodding. He dove straight down, until they were but thirty feet above them.

"FIRE!" she shrieked.

Theon opened his mouth and breathed before she uttered the command, the two thinking the same thing at the same time.

Down below, the trolls looked up, shock and terror in their eyes. They shrieked as Theon breathed a column of flame, cutting a swath of death right down the middle of their ranks. The great sound of flames merged with his roar, and he flew over them, for mile after mile, killing tens of thousands of trolls. More than one threw a spear or lance his way, but Theon was stronger now, and able to burn the weapons with the intense heat of his flames before they even reached him.

Finally, though, there came a hissing noise, and Kyra saw that Theon, still a baby, needed to replenish his fire. She took stock of what they had done, all the dead trolls, and was about to take pride in it, when she looked up ahead and saw an even bigger wave of trolls coming.

Her heart sank. Her attack had hardly made a dent. Escalon, she knew, was finished. She knew then that the only hope left would be for her to fulfill her mission.

"Higher, Theon!" she commanded.

Theon rose as the new wave of trolls hurled spears and lances into the sky; he flew higher and higher, just out of their reach, and soon they were back into the clouds. Kyra flew faster toward Marda. She closed her eyes and knew she needed to focus, to shake the visions from her mind. The only hope for her homeland, she knew, lay paradoxically farther north, deep in the heart of Marda.

*

Kyra felt the chill wrap around her shoulders, like a cloak of evil embracing her, as she entered the land of Marda. She felt an immediate shift in the air, something heavy and moist, like a dark spell pervading this place, gripping her, holding her tight. The sky immediately darkened, so much so that she was no longer able to tell if it were day or night. It hung there, in the gloom, not quite light and not quite dark, a perpetual twilight. Slivers of scarlet punctuated the thick, black clouds, as if the sky itself were bleeding.

Down below was hardly better. The landscape held no signs of life, just stretches of black dirt, ash, and outcroppings of black rock. There was no vegetation, no trees, and a myriad of volcanoes, molten lava pouring down the sides. She saw lakes of lava, and rivers of them cutting across the landscape in every direction.

Despite the lava, the land was cold—and it stank of sulfur—and the air was so thick with ash it was hard to breathe. Kyra could not have imagined anything worse in her darkest dreams. It looked like hell itself had found a place on earth.

As she flew, Kyra felt a deepening foreboding, a tightness in her chest. She had no idea where she was going, driven only by blind instinct, by the mandate of her mother, and she could not help but feel she would never return.

She scoured the landscape for a marker, any sign, any indication of where she should go. She searched for any road, something that might point her to the Staff of Truth. Yet she saw none.

The deeper into Marda she flew, the more lost she felt, wondering where to go in the vast and never-ending bleakness, wondering if she would ever even find what she was sent here for. Finally, as she looked down, she spotted something that caught her eye. It was movement, something in the landscape that stood out. It was gushing, black on black.

"Lower, Theon," she whispered.

Theon dove, and as they descended beneath the gloom of layers of clouds, she began to see more clearly. There below was a

69

gushing river of black, cutting through a landscape of blackness. It wound its way north, inexplicably uphill, through a narrow cut between two tall peaks.

As she watched it, Kyra sensed something lay on the far side of those mountains. She sensed in her heart that it was where she needed to go.

"Down, Theon."

Theon flew toward the peaks, Kyra planning to fly over them—yet as they neared, Theon suddenly, to her shock, screeched and came to a sudden stop in the air.

He flailed, and would not proceed.

"What is it, Theon?" she asked.

His words come to her in her head.

I cannot fly forward.

Kyra looked out and with a sense of dread realized there was some sort of invisible force here, a shield keeping Theon out. She looked down at the landscape, the gushing river, the mouth of it waiting below her, and she knew it was where she was meant to go. She needed to travel that river to the other side of those mountains, and it was a journey, she realized, she would have to take alone.

With a pang of panic, Kyra realized she would have to leave Theon here.

"Down, Theon," she said softly. "I will land."

Theon reluctantly heeded her, diving and touching down beside the mouth of the river. As she dismounted, she felt a creepy feeling beneath her feet as she stepped onto a soft, mossy landscape, all black.

Theon lowered his head, looking ashamed—and looking concerned for her.

Return with me, Theon said to her in her mind. *Let us leave this place together.*

Kyra slowly shook her head, stroking the scales on his long nose.

"I cannot," she said. "My destiny lies here. Fly south, and await me in Escalon."

Kyra looked over at the slow-moving river and saw a wide, black raft, made of logs tied together, waiting at the mouth of the river, as if only for her. On the raft stood a being, perhaps a man, perhaps some kind of evil creature, his back to her, wearing a black cloak, holding a long staff, its tip in the water. He did not turn to face her.

Theon lowered his head and pushed it against hers, and Kyra rubbed his scales and kissed him.

"Go, my friend," she commanded.

Theon finally screeched and leapt into the air, his great talons just missing her. He spread his wings wide and flew off, never looking back, his screech the only reminder that he was ever here. Soon, the sky was empty. Theon was gone.

Kyra turned, a pit in her stomach, and walked over to the raft. Slowly, she stepped foot on it.

It rocked as she did, unsteady beneath her feet, her heart pounding in her throat. She felt completely and utterly alone, more alone than she'd ever had in her life.

She gripped her staff tight.

"Let us go," she said to the creature, sensing it was awaiting her command.

Its back still to her, it reached forward with its staff and dragged the river's bottom, and soon they were off, their raft floating downriver, into the blackness—and into the very heart of hell.

CHAPTER SEVENTEEN

Softis made his way slowly through the ruins of Volis, picking his way with his staff, walking, remembering. He paused at the remnant of a wall and ran his hand along its edge, still smooth, and recalled playing here as a boy. He remembered, as a boy, knowing that Volis would last forever.

Softis recalled his father and grandfather, remembered playing at their feet, learning about all the great historians, the famed Chroniclers of the Kingdom who had traveled from Andros. He knew there was no higher calling, and he had known as soon as he could walk that it was what he was meant to do. For him, it was the histories that held the glory, not the waging of wars. Wars, after all, faded away, while the Chroniclers made them live forever.

Softis breathed deeply as he continued walking, his staff gently picking through rocks. He was alone now, utterly alone, everyone he knew and loved dead. For some strange reason he could not understand, he had been cursed with the mixed blessing of survival. And he had survived. He had survived his grandfather, his father, his wife, his siblings—and even all his children. He had survived kings and wars, one commander after the next. He had seen Escalon under many forms of rule, yet had never seen it entirely free. Nearly a hundred years old now, he had outlived it all.

Softis knew he could find a way to go on, a way to live without the men and women and children, whom he dearly missed but was nearly too blind to see now; he could live without the variety of food, finding a way to subsist only on foraged grasses and berries, food he was too old to truly taste anyway. But what he could not live without, what made him feel most alone of all, was the loss of his books. Those savages had destroyed them all, and in the process had torn apart his soul.

Well, not all of them. One book, hidden deep beneath a stone vault, Softis had hidden and salvaged. It was this book, The Chronicles of his Fathers, an oversized, leather-bound book with pages so worn from use that they nearly fell out, that Softis gripped to his chest now as he walked. It was all he had left to live for.

Escalon, he concluded, was haunted. It was both a blessed and a cursed land. It had always been haunted by the threat of dragons, the threat of trolls, the threat of Pandesia. It was a place of great beauty and yet, paradoxically, a place where one could never truly rest easy. There was some riddle to this land, something he could never quite figure out. He had been turning over the legends in his mind for nearly a hundred years, and there was something, he felt, that was missing. Something, perhaps, that was even withheld from him, some secret even too great for him, for his forefathers. What was it?

Perhaps it was contained in some missing book, some missing scroll, some missing legend he had not yet heard. There was something, he was convinced, that solved it all, that made sense of the mysterious origin of Escalon, and of what had both cursed and blessed it.

Now, as his eyes dimmed and he faced the waning of his life, it was no longer life he craved, but *knowledge*. Wisdom. The unraveling of secrets. And most of all, the answer to that mystery. Softis knew how history would end. It would end how all men ended. In death. In nothing. But he still did not know how the story *began*. And in some ways, in his eyes, that was more important.

Softis picked his way farther through the rubble, this ghost town filled only with the faint sound of his staff, of the gales of wind rushing through here and finding no one. Finding a small, old stale piece of bread, he reached down and picked it up, hard as a rock, wondering how many weeks it had sat there. Still, he was grateful for it, knowing it would be his best find of the day. It would give him energy enough, at least, for the walk. On his way to the mausoleum, he would visit old friends, immerse himself in old times. He would close his eyes and imagine his father alive with him again, telling him story after story. That comforted him. Indeed, he was more comforted by ghosts these days than by the living.

As he picked his way across the courtyard, Softis suddenly stopped and stood. He had felt something. Had it been a tremor?

He felt it again, running up through his staff to his palm, something so faint he wondered if it had even come. But then, sure enough, it came again. This time, the tremor was a shake, and then a rumble. He stopped, feeling it now in the soles of his feet, and he turned and looked up, out through the broken arch that was once the formidable gate to Volis.

There was something on the horizon. It was faint, at first, like a cloud of dust. But it grew as he watched. It became an outline, a dark shadow, an army forming on the horizon.

And then it became thunder.

A moment later, the stampede came. They came racing over the hill, sounding like a herd of buffalo. They filled the horizon, the shouts audible now even to his deaf ears. They charged and filled the barren hillside, all coming, he was amazed to see, right for Volis.

What could they want with Volis?

As they came closer, he realized there was nothing they wanted here. Volis merely had the bad fortune of standing in their way.

They charged through the gate, and finally, Softis could see them clearly. As he did, his heart froze in his chest. These were no humans. Nor were they Pandesians.

Trolls.

An entire nation of trolls.

Halberds raised high, shrieking, vicious, blood in their eyes, they swarmed the land like locusts, clearly determined to destroy every last blade of grass in Escalon, to leave no thing unturned. It was as if the gates of hell had been unleashed.

As Softis stood there, in the center of Volis, the last man left alive, he realized they were coming right for him. Finally, for the first time in his life, death had targeted him.

Softis did not run. He did not cower. Instead, he stood there proudly, and for the first time in his life, he did his best to raise his arched back so that he would stand straight and tall, as his father might have done.

The trolls thundered through the gates, halberds held high, lowering them right for him, and Softis clutched his book to his chest, and he smiled. The curse of his life was over.

Finally, he had been blessed with death.

CHAPTER EIGHTEEN

Dierdre and Marco hiked through the woods as they had for hours, falling into the monotony of rhythm, of silence, of leaves crunching beneath their feet, each lost in their own gloom. Dierdre tried to shake away the images that flashed through her mind—of her father's death, of Ur being flooded, of her nearly drowning beneath those waves. And yet every time she closed her eyes and shook her head, they only came back stronger. She saw herself tumbling through the water, saw her father's face, dead, lifeless, staring up at the sky. She saw her beloved city, all she knew in the world, completely underwater, now nothing more than another forgotten lake.

Dierdre looked out at the white, glistening trees of Whitewood, tried to focus on something else, anything, to take her mind off the past. She still felt herself trembling, so caught up in her past trauma that it was hard for her to even remember where she was. She forced herself to focus. Where was she? Where were they going?

She turned and saw Marco hiking beside her, and it came rushing back to her: Kyra. They were heading north, to the Tower of Ur, to find her.

Dierdre looked at Marco. With his strong chin, broad shoulders, and dark features, he stood much taller than she, and she took comfort in his presence. There was something about him— quiet, never boastful, quick to listen—that made it easy to be with. Most of all, he was always there, by her side, and she realized she could depend on him. He had become like a rock to her.

Seeing him made her think of Alec, of the feelings she had felt for his friend, and it brought up fresh feelings of betrayal at Alec's having fled. Had Alec survived? she wondered. If so, where was he now? If death was inevitable in this land, which it seemed it was, Dierdre could not help but wonder if it would have been better for Alec to die in glory with the others than to be dead somewhere else.

It all made her wonder who she could really trust in this world. Marco, she felt, was a man she could trust. In some ways, he reminded her of her father.

"And what if your friend is not there?"

Dierdre was startled by the broken silence. Marco was looking at her, too, clearly jolted from his own thoughts, black rings beneath his eyes. He looked exhausted, and she could only wonder what dark thoughts flooded his mind, too.

"She will be," Dierdre replied, confident. "Kyra wouldn't die. She is a survivor."

Marco shook his head.

"Perhaps you put too much faith in your friend," he said. "She is human, like us. How could she have survived the attack?"

"The Tower of Ur is far from the city," Dierdre said. "Perhaps they have not reached her yet. Besides, she's not alone. She has her horse and her wolf."

Marco scoffed.

"And they can stop an army?"

Dierdre frowned.

"Kyra has more than that," she added. "I can't explain it, but she is special. If anyone can survive this war, it would be her."

Marco shook his head.

"You speak as if she's a magical being."

Dierdre thought about that, and as he said the words, she realized there was some truth to them. There *was* something different about Kyra. She couldn't quite put her finger on it, but there was something about her that made her seem…special.

"Maybe she is," Dierdre finally said, wondering aloud even as she spoke the words.

"And if your friend is dead?" Marco pressed.

Dierdre sighed.

"Then we have journeyed north for nothing," she admitted. "Either way, we will reach the Tower of Ur, and find safety there. The Watchers will take us in."

"Why would they?" he asked.

"They must," she insisted. "They are a fellowship of the kingdom, after all, and we are under attack. If nothing else, they will give us food, shelter, and a place to stay as long as we need it. From there, we can decide."

He shook his head.

"Maybe you are right," he said, "but maybe you are not. Maybe we should head to the sea, find a boat, can get as far from Escalon as we can."

They continued hiking in silence, the only sound that of the leaves beneath their boots, each lost in their own thoughts. As more time passed, Dierdre began to feel how precarious their position was, how little time they might have left alive. She no longer felt the luxury of time, and she felt an urgency to know more about Marco.

"Tell me of your family," she said tentatively, almost afraid to ask. Normally she would not be so forthright, but she felt she had no time.

Marco glanced at her, then looked away as his face dropped.

"My family's been dead to me for most of my life," he said, with the gloom of a person who has never known and loved his family. "My father was cruel to me ever since I was born. My mother, well, he oppressed her, too, and she retreated into herself. That was how she dealt with it. I had always wanted to protect her. But I couldn't."

Dierdre began to realize the layers of sadness that forged Marco's character.

"I'm sorry," she said.

He shrugged.

"That is in the past," he said. "I feel that all the people we look up to betray us at one time or another. We must look for strength within ourselves, not hope to find it in others."

It made her think of her own father, of their oft-difficult relationship, and it made her realize that life was a mystery to her. Dierdre realized that she and Marco had more in common than she thought. They understood each other, in an odd way. Both of them had been raised without true love in their lives. Only now was she realizing what a horrible thing that was for a child.

"Neither of us deserved it," she finally said.

He nodded slowly as he walked.

"We don't always get we deserve," he replied. "Sometimes you must take what you deserve in life. Or sometimes you get it later in life, when you least expect it and least need it. But even if we don't get what we deserve in life, that doesn't mean we can't *end up* with what we deserve. We have the power to *decide* what we deserve in life. We have the power to let ourselves have it—even if other people say we don't deserve it."

He kicked at the leaves as he went.

"Mostly," he continued, "we must stop thinking in terms of deserve or not deserve. When we don't make demands on the world to give us what we think we deserve, we will find ourselves less disappointed. I'd rather create what I want in life than demand the world give me things. The former puts the power into my own hands; the latter strips it away and puts me at the mercy of the world."

Dierdre liked that. The more she thought about it, the more she realized he was right—and that Marco was a more profound person than she had realized.

"And what do *you* deserve in life, Marco?" she asked, feeling a greater respect for him.

"I deserve it all," he said firmly, sounding confident, without missing a beat—and she believed him. "And why shouldn't I?" he continued. "Why should I deserve any less than anyone else?"

He fell silent and looked to her.

"And you?" he asked, hesitant.

"I deserve love," she answered. "True love. After all, what is more powerful in life?"

He looked at her, then looked away, and he blushed. Dierdre could see in that moment that he had feelings for her. He *did* care for her; he was just too scared to say it. But she saw it in his eyes before he looked away.

They continued hiking in silence, drifting closer to each other, falling into a comfortable silence, as hours more passed.

Finally, they emerged from the wood, and as they did, they both stopped short, stunned at the sight before them. Dierdre's breath caught in her throat as she stared out at the landscape. The image seared itself on her soul—like something out of a nightmare.

There stood the Tower of Ur, not resplendent, as she had anticipated—but collapsed in a pile of rubble. She heard herself gasp. What could never be destroyed sat destroyed before her.

Seeing it, Dierdre felt as if something had collapsed within her. There lay the tower, one of the foundations of Escalon, destroyed.

Worse, Kyra was nowhere to be seen. Neither was Andor, or Leo. What awful force could have ripped through here and done this? she wondered.

Beyond it, in the distance, Kyra could see the Sea of Sorrow, and her heart fell to see its waters black with more Pandesian fleets—all sailing toward shore.

They each stood there in shock and total silence for several minutes. Dierdre felt that all of her dreams, her hopes for safe haven, were crushed. It seemed there was no place safe anymore. Most of all, she was filled with sadness for her friend. There was no way Kyra could have survived this. She must be dead, too. And that left no hope for her.

"It's not possible," Dierdre heard herself say aloud.

Marco seemed too stunned to say anything.

Dierdre felt a tremor—and suddenly there came a tremendous shout from the woods. She turned and stared with dread at the woodline, and watched in horror as there burst forth an army of trolls. They came charging out at her, disfigured, grotesque, huge, halberds raised high, and running right for her.

Dierdre reached out and grabbed Marco's hand and squeezed tight. There was little he could do but squeeze back. The trolls were hardly fifty yards away, closing in fast, and Dierdre knew in that moment that, for some cruel reason, fate had allowed them to survive the flood—only to die by a much worse fate.

CHAPTER NINETEEN

Duncan, flanked by Kavos, Bramthos, Seavig and Arthfael, trailed by Motley and Cassandra, led his army as they marched across the plains, heading south, away from the shelter of the cave, and somewhere toward the Canyon of Baris. Duncan shifted in his armor, sweating, oppressed by the midday heat, their march feeling as if it had taken days. The entire army's armor rattled, its perpetual clinking the only thing breaking the silence of this long, barren stretch of Escalon.

There was no shade to be found, nothing here but rock and dirt and the hope of their destination. It was a risky, exposed march, and yet Duncan knew they had no choice—they had to get as far away from the capital as they could, had to distance themselves from the Pandesian army and reach Baris before it was too late. They had to protect their flank. And Duncan had a score to settle.

Duncan's blood boiled as he thought of Bant, the great traitor. The coward lived on, after selling out Duncan, clearly having sealed a pact with the Pandesians. Duncan would teach him the meaning of betraying his fellow countrymen. He would give him a visit he would never forget, and avenge all the lost lives of his men.

As he marched, Duncan thought of his son Aidan, and wondered if he had been wrong to allow him to join Anvin on the mission to Leptus. He was so young, and yet he had proved himself, and was determined. The time came for all boys, Duncan knew, to become men. And yet that was a crucial mission, one that could determine whether his own army would succeed. The men of Leptus might not feel compelled to join the cause, and if they would not come, Duncan knew that his men could find themselves fighting a losing battle in the canyon.

Duncan had bigger problems. He could feel the loss of morale amongst his men, having lost so many of their brothers on all the campaigns since Volis. Now here they were again, trekking across this endless landscape only to hope for more battle. It would be a battle, if they even won, that would only protect their flank and set them up to fight yet another battle. With dragons circling and the Pandesians filling his land, an end seemed nowhere in sight.

Duncan could not help but admit to himself that he had doubts, too. Escalon, it seemed, would never be free again.

Yet Duncan knew from his experience that numbers did not tell the entire story; if he could strike the Pandesians at the right moment, could take them by surprise using the vantage point of his homeland's terrain, maybe, just maybe, he could drive them into a trap and kill enough of them. If he could just drive them back to the Devil's Gulch, he could seal them off, and from there, maybe even find a way to take the Bridge of Sorrows. He recalled all the legends, stories of a few brave warriors, well positioned, holding the Devil's Gulch against thousands. It would soon be time to put that to the test—if he even made it that far.

Most of all, Duncan's troubled thoughts turned to Kyra. His heart lifted with pride as he recalled her flying on Theon, saving him and his men from the burning capital. He had never been more proud of her. He cringed inside as he thought of her flying to Marda, a place from which no man had ever ventured. His heart sank as he wondered if he'd ever see her face again.

Duncan's thoughts were jolted by a sound. At first he thought it was thunder behind them, but when he turned, he did a double take as he saw the horizon filled with black.

Heart pounding, Duncan stopped and turned with the rest of his army—and as he did, a chorus of Pandesian horns suddenly filled the air. There, pursuing them, were tens of thousands of Pandesian soldiers, leaving the capital, marching south. Led, in a procession of golden chariots, by Ra.

Many of the Pandesians rode horses, while some even rode elephants, and they sounded the horns again and again, a sound designed to strike panic into the enemy's hearts. It was effective, making it hard to think straight.

Duncan could feel all the eyes on him, all his men looking to him for guidance. The Pandesians had shown up too quickly, before he could reach the safety of the canyon, before he could secure his flank and lure them into his trap. Duncan turned and saw, on the horizon, the contours of the canyon, too far to reach in time.

He turned and faced the incoming Pandesians and knew he would have to fight them here, now, a much greater army, in the open plain. He summed it up with his professional eye, and he knew in an instant that there was no way his men, however valiant, could win.

"Commander?" came a voice.

Duncan turned to see Kavos standing beside him, awaiting his command with all his warriors. He came to a decision. He turned to Kavos and spoke in his most authoritative voice.

"Take our men and continue south, for the canyon. I shall take a small group and face off against this army myself, long enough to distract them, to give you time to make the canyon safely. It shall give you time to defeat Baris, to hold the canyon and defend yourselves."

Kavos looked back solemnly.

"And you?" he asked gravely.

Duncan shook his head.

"I will do what every commander must do," he replied. "I shall die with honor and save the bulk of my men."

His men all stared back, somber.

Finally, Kavos stepped forward.

"A noble choice, Duncan," he said. "But we shall not let you make a last stand alone."

"It is not a request," Duncan replied, "but a command. The men need someone to lead them. Take them and save them."

"Name someone else," Kavos replied, drawing his sword, standing beside Duncan to defend him. "Name anyone other than I."

"And I," Bramthos said, drawing his sword and joining them, too.

All around him brave men drew their swords, joining him, having his back, and Duncan was filled with gratitude and respect for them all.

Finally, seeing they would not budge, Duncan nodded to Arthfael.

"Very well then," he said. "You, Arthfael. Lead the bulk of this army to the canyon. Secure it, and win a victory for us all."

Arthfael hesitated for a moment, then finally nodded and followed his command. A horn sounded, and in moments he was off, leading nearly all of Duncan's men forward for the canyon.

Duncan turned and faced the Pandesian army, a dozen of his men by his side, holding their swords bravely—and he himself drew his sword. Death was marching for him, and he felt not fear, but relief. At least he would die nobly, for a cause, as he had always hoped to.

"Men," Duncan said, "shall we wait for them to reach us? Or shall we bring the war to them?"

His men all cheered, and as one, all these brave warriors followed him, racing into the desert landscape, swords raised high, Duncan feeling the familiar rush of adrenaline as he knew a glorious battle, perhaps the last of his life, awaited him.

CHAPTER TWENTY

Merk stood on the cliffs of the isle of Knossos, alongside hundreds of fierce warriors who glared out to the sea, as if to challenge whatever it brought them. He glanced over his shoulder and was reassured to see behind him the tall, stone fort of Knossos, rising out of the rock, and in its narrow windows, the glowing yellow eyes of dozens of Watchers, watching the battle with hoods drawn close over their heads. Hundreds more soldiers stood on its battlements. At the very top of the fort, standing atop the parapets, he spotted Lorna, standing there proudly, watching over it all from above.

He turned and looked back out at the black waters, filled with Vesuvius' ships, a nation of trolls sailing steadily their way. They were small ships, and they filled the bay, rocking on its currents, making their way ever closer. The relentless waves of the Bay of Death crashed into the rocks, their white spray shooting up into the air, moistening tops of the rocks, Merk and his weapons wet with spray. The wind had picked up to a driving gale, as if a perpetual storm were on the way, and hadn't slowed since.

Merk tightened his grip on his new weapon, the long chain with the spiked ball dangling to his feet, and his heart beat faster as he braced himself. Sailing to the drumbeats of war, the trolls were hardly a hundred yards away now and approaching fast, the currents bringing them closer with each breath, as if carrying demons from hell.

Merk looked about and was reassured to see all the proud warriors of Knossos, with their strong, square faces, their pale skin, their long beards streaked with gray, all staring at the sea, all unflinching. All held onto their long chains, spiked balls at the end, and he could not see a trace of fear in any of them. On the contrary, they looked as if they were looking out at the waters on a normal clear day, watching them with only a passing interest. Merk could not understand the complexities of these men, their deep reservoir of courage. It was as if, for them, life and battle were one.

"LONG CHAINS, ADVANCE!" their commander suddenly called in a booming voice able to be heard above the wind and the waves.

As one, the well-disciplined army advanced in rows, a great rattle of armor and chains filling the air, stepping past Merk to the very edge of the rock.

At the same time, the first dozen ships rushed forward in the currents, rising and falling in the waves of the Bay of Death, the trolls scowling, their grotesque faces now visible up close. They came within a dozen yards of shore, clearly preparing to disembark on the shores of Knossos, while the Knossos warriors awaited the next command. Merk stood there, palms sweating despite the cold, wondering how long their commander would wait as this nation invaded.

"FORWARD!" the commander finally cried.

His soldiers stepped forward, raised their long chains high overhead, and swung them around in broad circles. They whistled in the air, a chorus of high-pitched noises as the chains extended in broad arcs, stretching out a good twenty feet. They swung them expertly, so as not to hit each other—and then finally they swung them straight down.

Merk was shocked at what he saw next: the balls dove down, twenty feet in front of them, and smashed down below, into the hulls of the ships. A cracking noise filled the air as the spiked balls smashed the ships to pieces.

The boats, gaping holes in them, keeled over, then immediately sank into the bay.

The trolls, caught off guard, fell into the treacherous waters, weighed down by their armor, and, flailing, immediately sank into the raging currents of the Bay of Death.

The next row of ships advanced in the currents, and these trolls looked up in panic, realizing it was too late for them to turn back. With the currents as strong as they were, they couldn't slow their advance if they tried.

Once again the soldiers of Knossos stepped forward, swung their chains, and smashed the hulls.

These ships, too, sank.

Another row of ships advanced—and another was smashed to pieces.

Row after row of ships were destroyed, and before long, the waters were filled with smashed ships, their debris smashing into the rocks.

Merk grinned as he watched hundreds of trolls flail and sink in the rapid waters. Yet he heard a snarl, and he looked up to see their leader, Vesuvius, standing at the bow of his ship, in the midst of his fleet, scowling back and pointing. He was still a good hundred yards from shore, far enough away to stop his momentum.

"BOWS!" cried Vesuvius.

Within moments hundreds of trolls raised their bows, and arrows filled the air.

The wind coming off the Bay of Death carried the arrows every which way, many of them falling short, down to the rocks, into the water. But enough of them sailed through, and they fell for the warriors of Knossos.

Thurn was prepared, though.

"SHIELDS!"

Dozens of his men rushed forward, held up huge shields, and came together, elbow to elbow, blocking the arrows in a perfect line of a discipline. Merk knelt beside them, as one handed him a shield.

More and more arrows fell, and each time they were stopped by this wall of bronze.

"SPEARS!" Vesuvius shrieked, from his wildly rocking ship.

Trolls hurled a host of long, glistening spears, soaring in a high arc above the shields, heading for the body of Knossos warriors. But the warriors, well-trained, reacted immediately.

"SHORT CHAINS!"

The soldiers pulled short chains from their waists and swung, and the spiked balls at the end smashed the spears from the sky before they could hit.

Vesuvius, enraged, grabbed a spear himself and chucked it low and hard, straight for Thurn.

Thurn just stood there, unfazed, and as the spear came, he merely swung his chain and ball and smashed the spear out of the sky.

Vesuvius sounded the horns, and as he did, dozens of his ships converged in a line, single file. They sailed forward, and as the first reached shore, the warriors of Knossos smashed it. Yet while they were able to reach the ship behind it, Vesuvius took advantage, reaching out himself and grabbing one of the chains after it came down.

86

He yanked, and the Knossos soldier fell off the cliffs, face-first into the water.

The other trolls all joined in, following Vesuvius, all rushing forward and grabbing the chains; they caught the warriors of Knossos off guard as they yanked, sending one man after the next down into the bay.

"CHARGE!" Vesuvius yelled.

So much debris had backed up in the crashing waves that Vesuvius was able to use them as a bridge for the last few feet to shore, jumping from one plank to the next, rocking in the water as he leapt for the rocky shore. All around him his men did the same. Vesuvius used the chain he had snatched, swinging it himself, a handy weapon which he quickly used to entangle several more chains and send dozens more warriors down into the waters below.

Hundreds of trolls charged onto the rocky shores, scrambling up the cliffs like goats and heading right for the rows of soldiers—and right for Merk.

Merk swung wildly into the onslaught of trolls, standing side by side with the soldiers, fighting back against the never-ending stream. A particularly large troll with hideous fangs charged him, raising his halberd and lowering it for Merk's head—and Merk sidestepped at the last second, swung around, and smashed the spiked ball into his head, killing him.

Merk stepped forward and kicked another troll in the chest as it climbed the rocks for him, halberd high, and sent it flying back down into the waters below. He looked over and watched it fall, and as he did, a wave of panic overtook him: hundreds of trolls were now on shore, and hundreds more were landing by the second. The ships clogged the bay, all of them smashing against the rocks, creating such a logjam that the trolls could storm it. Some ships were still smashed by the warriors of Knossos, but dozens slipped through the ranks.

Shoulder to shoulder with trolls, the fighting became hand-to-hand. Merk swung his chain and smashed the heads of two trolls as they neared. Yet more came, and as the fighting grew thicker, Merk realized he no longer had room to swing his chain. Four trolls charged him at once.

Unable to swing his chain, he instead grabbed it with both fists, sidestepped as a troll swung a halberd for his chest, then snuck behind the troll and wrapped the chain around his throat from behind. He quickly spun, holding the troll hostage, choking him, and faced the other three. One lunged with his sword and Merk used the hostage as a shield, forcing the troll to kill his friend. He then dropped him and kicked the shocked troll back over the cliff.

Merk drew his dagger as the other two approached and sliced one troll's throat. He leaned back and kicked the other, sending him flying back over the edge—but this troll, floundering, reached out and managed to grab hold of Merk's boot and pull him down with him.

Merk, caught off guard, hit the ground hard and began to slide over the edge with the troll. Panicking, halfway over the edge, Merk wheeled, grabbed onto a root, and held on for dear life.

Merk found himself dangling over the edge of the cliff, the troll hanging on, yanking on his foot from below. Merk, losing his grip, knew he needed to act fast. He picked his other leg up high, then kicked down with his other foot. He connected with the troll's nose, and finally the troll released his grip and fell shrieking to his death below.

Merk pulled himself back up, one hard pull at a time, until finally he collapsed on flat stone, out of breath. He looked up and saw dozens of Knossos warriors fighting valiantly, swinging their chains, smashing trolls in the face and neck and shoulders and ribs, smashing away their halberds and shields, fighting like men on fire. They had few men compared to this nation of trolls, and yet they did tremendous damage, holding their ground, filling the air with the sound of their whistling chains, the *thwack* of the metal balls hitting armor. They were warriors to be feared, unlike any Merk had ever seen. Single-handedly, they were stopping the tide of an army.

Yet for every troll they killed, three more appeared, a never-ending parade of these creatures from the sea. And soon enough, the men of Knossos, only human, began to fall.

First there came one—then another—then as Merk turned and looked, he saw the warriors being swarmed and overwhelmed from all directions. In no time, the tide turned, and their situation became dire.

Horns sounded, and Merk looked out to sea and saw hundreds more ships arriving. They were disembarking faster than he could count, ascending the cliffs like goats, and Merk felt a pit in his stomach as he soon realized that the men of Knossos would be no more.

Merk looked up and saw Lorna standing before the door to the fort, flanked by warriors who fought back the trolls, led by Thurn. She beckoned him, and Merk knew he had to reach her—or die.

Merk let out a guttural cry as he jumped to his feet and fought his way through the crowd. He grabbed a halberd off the ground and hacked his way through, felling trolls left and right with big, mighty swings. When his shoulders tired and the fighting became too close, he drew his dagger and used it expertly, bringing back his assassin days, cutting through these creatures as he ducked and weaved and stabbed expertly. Finally, he felt his skills being put to use for Escalon.

Merk stabbed and slashed and dodged his way all the way through the lines and back to the entrance to the fort, guarded by an arched wooden door. Finally, he reached Lorna's side. She stood surrounded by warriors, who swung chains and fought back the trolls valiantly.

"Have we any chance?" he called out to her, fighting back two trolls, crying out to be heard over the din.

She stared out at the sea and the sky, inexplicably calm.

"But one," she replied. "Yet it is far more dangerous than this."

"More than this?" he asked, shocked.

"The dragons," she said, turning to him. "I can summon them."

He looked at her in shock, swallowing hard, realizing.

"I, and the Watchers here, together. We can bring them. But we can't control them."

Merk looked out at the never-ending stream of trolls, and he realized their options were bleak. If they didn't do something, they would surely die at these beasts' hands.

She looked back at him silently with her crystal-blue eyes, and finally, he nodded back his approval.

Lorna turned and looked up at the fort, raising her palms high overhead, and as she did, dozens of Watchers, their yellow eyes shining, stuck their heads out of the narrow windows, reached out, and raised their palms to the sky, too.

There came a great humming noise, rising even over the din of the battle, of the wind, of the crashing waves. It soon dominated the very fabric of the air, the sound of Lorna and dozens of Watchers humming together, eyes closed, faces raised to the sky.

Suddenly, the sky rumbled with thunder and lightning, and a moment later, the battle stopped on both sides as everyone froze and searched the skies. There followed an awful roar, louder even than the thunder, as the skies parted and from their midst there suddenly appeared a host of dragons, ferocious, horrible, enraged, all opening their great jaws and diving down right for them.

It was, Merk knew, death coming for them all.

CHAPTER TWENTY ONE

Kyra stood unsteadily on the small raft, watching the sluggish, black river pass by below her as she wound her way silently, deeper into the heart of darkness. The creature behind her kept his head down and dragged his pole along the river floor, the gentle splashing the only sound punctuating the thick and gloomy silence. The deeper into Marda she went, the more her sense of unease deepened. She felt as if she were being led in a funeral procession to her death.

The air here was hot and moist, sticking to her like glue, the sky stuck in twilight, the only sound in this land that of distant explosions of volcanoes, of the hissing of the streams of lava that cut through the black mountainside. This land was all shades of black: the black sky, the black waters of the river, the black soil and ash of the countryside, and the two towering black mountains which loomed before her.

Kyra looked up with hesitation as the river carried her between the mountains, feeling claustrophobic. Each rose hundreds of feet high, black as ink, and as she looked closely, she saw thousands of tiny yellow eyes appearing in their crags, tiny creatures watching her as she passed. They looked like a thousand small stars in the night sky. She braced herself, wondering if they would pounce as she went.

Kyra tightened her grip on her staff, wishing she were anywhere but here. She had never felt so alone. She peered into the horizon, wondering where these waters were taking her, and sensing that wherever it was, it was leading her to the Staff of Truth. She felt she was being led to it, and yet she also sensed it was a trap. Yet she had little choice. She had no other beacons in this foreign and hostile land.

Kyra sensed a massive battle coming, a battle of spiritual forces, and she closed her eyes and felt a slight burning in her stomach. She knew that where she was going would test all that she had, all that she was, would force her to face the darkest parts of herself. She would rather battle a thousand men in an open field than grapple in this realm of darkness, a realm she did not entirely understand. It was the realm that held the key to saving Escalon, a realm of spirits, a realm of hidden powers. A realm of shadows.

The river finally led her out to the other side of the mountains, and as it did, the landscape opened up again. Kyra looked out into the countryside and this time spotted thousands of small, black structures, looking like clay cottages, abandoned. This seemed to be one of the cities of the troll nation, all deserted when the trolls fled south, for Escalon. Now Marda sat empty, awaiting their return, if ever. Lucky for her, Kyra realized—or else she would be battling thousands of trolls right now, on her way north.

Kyra studied the city as she passed through it, the endless cottages all the same, the streets of dirt, and she recoiled at what she saw: the black ground was littered with bones. There were bones everywhere, carcasses of rotting animals, all, she realized, the trolls' victims. It looked as if the trolls ate these creatures and then just left the bones on the ground. She also spotted fresh bodies on spikes, and realized the trolls slowly ate away at them. A savage nation.

Amongst these, Kyra spotted grotesque troll heads on pikes everywhere she looked, and she wondered if these trolls had been killed as a warning, because they had defied some sort of law, or if this was just some sort of sport. She felt sick as she saw some human heads amongst them, too, and wondered if these were the innocent victims kidnapped during their expeditions into Escalon.

The river turned, and Kyra recoiled as she saw an entire field of human bodies, dead, chained to each other. She gasped. Slaves. Poor, innocent humans the trolls had abducted when raiding Escalon, humans who'd had the bad fate to live a horrible, awful life here as slaves of these creatures, before finally meeting a miserable end. Kyra tightened her grip on her staff, determined to avenge them. A part of her wished all the trolls were here now, so she could battle them herself. No, she knew. A much worse battle was awaiting her.

Hearing an explosion on the horizon, Kyra forced herself to look away and instead focused on the huge ball of lava shooting into the air, sending thousands of streaks of bright light into the gloomy landscape. There arose a gentle clacking noise, and she looked down into the waters and was horrified to see they were sailing past bones, all floating downriver, bouncing gently off the raft, first a few, then dozens of them. They were of all shapes and sizes, and she tried not to wonder whose they were, or how they had got here.

Kyra thought of her mother, needing her strength. She pondered her words: *You must empty your mind, Kyra. You must unlearn everything you know.* What had she meant? *It is you, Kyra. It is you who must go there and retrieve the weapon.*

Had her mother been right? Did Escalon's salvation really lie here, in this hell? Had she ever even truly seen her mother? Or had it all been a dream?

Mother, Kyra called out in her mind. *Where are you? Are you with me?*

Kyra listened, quieting her mind, hoping to hear back. Yet nothing came but silence. It was as if the silence of Marda were too thick to penetrate, as if Kyra had gone too far to the ends of the world for her mother, for anyone, to be with her now.

She tried to focus, to draw strength from herself. What was it that Alva had once said to her? *To complete your training, first, you must forego the illusion that others are with you. You are born alone and you will die alone, and what you seek will come not from leaning on others, but on yourself. How deeply have you looked inside, Kyra? How deeply have you trusted yourself?*

Here, now utterly alone, Kyra was beginning to sense the truth of his words. And it began to dawn on her that this utter loneliness was what she needed to complete her training. She had been leaning on others for too long; this would force her to lean on herself. This was, she realized, the final leg of her training.

The river turned again, and Kyra's heart quickened as she watched the landscape change. Replacing the barren fields of dirt and ash, up ahead she saw a forest, a thick and tangled wood, stretching across the horizon as far as the eye could see. She saw huge thorns protruding from them, making the forest resemble one massive thorn bush. As they neared, she saw the trees themselves were sharp, thick, with gnarled, tangled branches, all black, devoid of foliage, devoid of life. At the entrance to this wood stood a narrow opening, a natural arch grown out of the thorns, allowing a single person entry into this foreboding place. And at the foot of this arch, the river came to an end.

Kyra felt her raft suddenly come to a stop, beaching on the shore before the wood. She stepped off, exchanging one foreboding surface for another, and wondering which was worse.

Kyra looked back to thank the person who had brought her—yet as she did, she was shocked to see the raft was already far away, floating downriver—and on it, there was nobody. Her sense of foreboding deepened. What was this land?

Kyra began to walk toward the entrance to the wood, knowing this was where she needed to go, and she had hardly gone a few feet when suddenly, the black soil before her shot up in an explosion.

Kyra recoiled and stepped back, on guard, as there emerged from the very soil itself, a massive, grotesque monster. It grew taller and taller, forming itself out of the ash, taking on the shape of a man, a grotesque man, three times the size of any man she'd known. It was a giant, shoulders three times as broad, with sharp daggers for fingers, claws for toes. He had spikes sticking out of his rib cage, and his head was large and misshapen, with three orange eyes and razor-sharp fangs for teeth.

She glanced down and for the first time noticed a pile of bones at its feet, and she realized: other sojourners. He was the guardian. No one got past him.

The monster reared and roared, its muscles and veins bulging, a roar sharp enough to shake the world. It raised its claws, and suddenly rushed her.

Kyra had to think quick. The beast sliced its claws down for her head, surprisingly fast, and she let her reflexes take over, ducking at the last second. Its claws whooshed by her, just missing, slicing off some of her hair, which fell in locks down into the mud at her feet.

Next, it swung backwards the other way, faster than she could anticipate, and she barely ducked in time, the claws grazing her cheek. She was struck with a sharp pain as the claws scratched her and drew blood. Yet, luckily, the main force of the swing had missed her, and Kyra, regaining herself, raised her staff, swung around, and cracked its wrist.

The beast roared in pain—yet it backhanded her in the same motion, and she went flying, airborne, up twenty feet, landing on her back in the mud.

Kyra, winded, backed up as it bore down on her. Its footsteps shook the earth as it sprinted right for her. She had nowhere to go, she realized in a panic, slipping as she backed up in the mud.

Kyra closed her eyes, sensing death approaching, and focused internally. She could not physically overpower this beast. She needed to summon her power. She needed to transcend the physical world.

Kyra felt a sudden burning in her palms, and feeling her power rising up within, she raised her hands. As the beast neared her, she held them out before her.

Two glowing balls of energy shot forth, smashing the beast in the chest and knocking it on its back.

It roared, and a second later, to her shock, it bounded back onto its feet and charged her again.

Please, God, she thought. *Give me the strength to leap over this beast.*

Kyra took two steps, running for it, and leapt into the air, praying her powers would not fail her now. If they did, she would die in its awful embrace.

To her immense relief, she found herself leaping up, higher and higher into the air. She leapt over its head, as the beast ran right past her, and landed on the other side of it. As she did, she wheeled and cracked it on the back with her staff.

It stumbled and fell face-first in the mud.

The beast looked back at her, seemingly stunned. Kyra, emboldened, would not give it time to regroup.

She charged forward to finish it off, yet as she did, it surprised her, swinging back around at the last second and knocking her legs out from under her.

As she landed on her back, it spun, made a fist, and raised it high, preparing to smash her into the ground.

Kyra rolled out of the way at the last second, its hammer-fist leaving a huge crater in the earth, just missing her.

She rolled as he hammered again and again, just missing each time, until finally she raised her staff, twisted it, and split it in two, revealing the concealed blades, grabbing one end in each hand. She raised it high, and as the beast struck, she rolled out of the way and plunged the two blades into the beast's hand, pinning it to the earth.

The beast shrieked, stuck, unable to free itself.

Yet it surprised her by reaching over with its free hand and grabbing her by the throat. It squeezed her neck so fast and so tight, she was certain she would die.

Unable to breathe, Kyra gasped in agony, while the beast swung her left and right, shaking her until she felt sure she was about to die. It then he brought her toward its open mouth, opening it wider and wider as if to bite off her head.

Kyra closed her eyes and forced herself to focus not on what was before her, but on the energy coursing within.

You are stronger than this beast, she willed herself to believe. *You are stronger than all forces outside of you. They all inhabit the world of illusion. The only world that is real is that inside of you.*

Kyra slowly felt the certainly of her thoughts, felt them morph into beliefs, into what she knew was true. As she did, she felt her palms get burning hot. She opened her eyes and raised her palm and knew without fail that a white orb of light would come shooting forth, would save her.

It did. It flew through the air and smashed the beast in the mouth—and as it did, the beast went flying backwards, releasing its grip, the force so powerful that its other hand, impaled in the ground, came free. It flew a good twenty feet through the air, until finally it crashed onto the ground and lay there, dead.

Kyra, finally free, gasped for air. She saw the creature lying there, and she began to feel a great sense of power. She *did* have power. She was growing stronger in this place, she could feel it. With no turning back and no one to fall back on, she was learning how to become herself, how to master herself. There was something, too, about the darkness of this place that egged her on. Was she transforming into something else?

Kyra went to the wood before her and stood before the arched entrance. She felt it beckoning her, leading her deeper into darkness. Now she no longer feared it.

Now she craved it.

CHAPTER TWENTY TWO

Aidan galloped across the barren landscape, Anvin beside him, White at their heels, sweating, the sun bearing down on them. He gasped for air, the dust in his face making it hard to breathe. Somewhere on the horizon, he knew, was Leptus, and as exhausted as he was, he forced himself to hang in there, to not show any weakness, especially in front of Anvin. They had been riding for hours, not even pausing to take a break since they had left his father and his men back outside Andros, and Aidan was determined not to let them down. He wanted Anvin to think of him as a man now.

As they rode, Aidan was filled with a sense of pride, and of urgency. This, he knew, was the most important mission of his life, and he was thrilled his father had allowed it. He knew the stakes could not be higher: If he and Anvin failed, if the men of Leptus refused to join in the battle against Baris, his father and his men would certainly die.

That gave him strength. Aidan ignored his pain, his exhaustion, his hunger, the heat of the sun, and rode on and on, taking strength from Anvin beside him, who, despite being wounded, despite his heavy armor, never slowed once. On the contrary, Anvin rode with an erect posture, the very embodiment of selflessness and valor.

They rode and rode, the sound of the horses thundering in Aidan's ears, the sun arcing in the sky, the afternoon shadows growing stronger. Aidan was convinced that they would never reach Leptus.

And then, suddenly they crested a hill, and the landscape began to shift. The rock and desert, the endless rows of tumbleweed, began to give way to soil, to grass, to trees; the endless flat monotony gave way, on the horizon, to shapes, to structures. They soon passed an occasional clay dwelling, and then these became more and more frequent, packed more densely together. And soon, in the landscape, there appeared a road—and this road, Aidan saw with delight and relief, led to a stronghold.

Aidan was impressed to see a medium-size city perched at the edge of the desert, nestled along the shores of the Bay of Death. He held up a hand and squinted, the glare so strong off the glistening waters behind it.

Leptus. They had made it.

Leptus was a minor city, he knew, in the southern reaches of Escalon, the southernmost city on this side of Everfall. South of Baris but north of Thebus, Leptus was known as the last real city of the south. It was so out of the way, here in this arid landscape, so far from anywhere, it was known as a hard place, an outpost, a place of separatists. It lacked the lush, verdant rolling hills of most of Escalon, and being here in this hard place, sandwiched between the desert and Everfall and the Bay of Death, made Aidan glad that he had been raised in Volis.

Yet ironically, this small stronghold, so far from all the major trade routes and roads, so hard to get to, had become the last holdout for the free men of Escalon. Here resided the last free warriors, the only men left whom the Pandesian invasion had not yet reached. Of course, Aidan knew, it was only because of their geography, and soon enough, that would change. Yet for now, it made these men of Leptus the last people his father could turn to for help.

They continued down the road for the city, and soon Aidan found himself riding over a small, stone bridge, crossing an inlet of the Bay of Death, black waters swirling beneath them. They rode on, Aidan's heart pounding with excitement, until they finally reached a large, arched stone gate, its iron portcullis lowered, and a dozen fierce warriors standing before it. They stood at perfect attention, wielding long halberds and looking straight ahead, wearing the same blue and white armor of their city's banner flying overhead.

Finally, Aidan and Anvin came to a stop before them, White at their feet, all breathing hard. Aidan wiped the dust off his face from the long ride.

The lead soldier, a tall, broad-shouldered man with a scar running down his right cheek, stepped forward and peered out at them.

"State your name," he demanded.

"Anvin," Anvin replied breathlessly, "of Volis. Duncan's commander. Here with me is Aidan, his son."

The man nodded back, cold and hard.

"And I am Leifall," he replied. "What business you have in Leptus?"

98

Anvin took a deep breath.

"We are men of Escalon," Anvin called back, breathing hard, "and have come on urgent business. Open these gates at once and bring us to your commander."

Leifall stared back, unmoved.

"What business?" he demanded.

"The fate of Escalon," Anvin called back.

Yet still, Leifall did not step aside.

"Who sent you?" he demanded.

"Duncan of Volis," Anvin replied.

Leifall, with his elongated face and the narrow eyes of the people of the south, slowly rubbed his brown beard.

"First I must know: what is your business here?" he asked, his voice still hard.

"Bring me to be your commander, and I will tell him myself," Anvin called back, impatient.

Leifall stared back, hard, unmoving.

"*I* am the commander here," he said.

They stared back in surprise.

"*You?*" Anvin said. "Why would a commander be guarding a gate?"

The commander stared back, hard and cold.

"*He who leads must stand first in peril.* That is our motto," he replied. "Where else should a commander be?" he called back. "The people of Leptus are a democratic people. I ask nothing of them I would not do myself. I stand with my men, and they with me. That is what makes us who we are."

He examined Anvin, while Aidan looked back at him with a whole new sense of respect.

"So I ask you again: what do you want of the men of Leptus?" Leifall called out.

Anvin dismounted, Aidan following his lead, relieved to be off the horse, and as they did, all the soldiers tensed, gripping their halberds as if to strike. The commander gestured to his men and they lowered their weapons, while White, snarling, came up beside Aidan, as if to defend him. Aidan stroked his head, putting him at ease.

Stopping a few feet away from the commander, Anvin spoke, his voice urgent.

"Our great country has been overrun," he said. "Perhaps you have not noticed because you reside here, out of the way from the rest of us. Pandesia has invaded. Escalon has fallen—all of it except for your little corner. Soon enough, they will march on Leptus, too."

Leifall looked back, skeptical, hardened, his eyes widening just a bit in surprise as he slowly rubbed his beard.

"Go on," he finally replied.

"Duncan rides for Baris now," Anvin continued. "He needs to destroy those who betrayed us, and to lure the Pandesians into the canyon. He needs your help."

The commander stroked his beard for a long time as he stood there, seemingly deep in thought, studying Anvin.

"And why should we help you?" he finally asked.

"Why?" Anvin asked, surprised. "Is not our cause your cause? Do we not share a homeland? A common invader?"

Leifall shook his head.

"Since when have you come to Leptus?" he replied. "And since when have we ventured to Volis? We may live on the same land, but we are different people, from different corners of a land, who merely share a capital."

Anvin narrowed his eyes.

"Is that the way of the men of Leptus then?" he asked. "To isolate themselves? To ignore their brothers in their time of need?"

Leifall reddened.

"You are no brother to me," he replied, his jaw locked. "Why should I risk my men to save this Duncan, this commander whom I have never met? Who has never bothered to pay homage to us once?"

Anvin frowned.

"He would help you if you came to him," he replied.

"Perhaps," the commander replied. "And perhaps not."

Anvin frowned, clearly frustrated.

"You would also be helping yourselves," he replied, "if that is all that matters. Do not think you will be spared by Pandesia."

Leifall shrugged, unimpressed.

"We have our own defenses," he replied. "We can fight on our own terms, and last much longer than you think. No one has ever taken these walls. And we have an escape route on the Bay of

Death. We are protected on both sides. This is why Leptus has never been taken."

"Do not flatter yourselves," Anvin countered, clearly upset. "Leptus has never been taken because you are so far out of the way, and because there is nothing of worth here."

Leifall scowled, and Aidan could feel the exchange quickly deteriorating.

"Call it what you will," the commander replied, "yet we are free and you are not."

"For now," Anvin replied.

Leifall breathed for a long time, seething, until finally he continued.

"Duncan's taking Baris is a poor strategy," he added. "No one takes the low ground. It is a death trap."

Anvin was undeterred.

"It is the best place to take shelter from the capital," he replied. "Andros is burning. The Pandesians are unfamiliar with Baris, and we can use the canyon to our advantage."

Leifall looked out into the distance, and after a long time, he sighed.

"Perhaps," he finally said. "Still, the men of Leptus would be better served fighting Pandesia here, on our own ground, with our own defenses, and with our backs to the Bay of Death. My job is to protect my people, not yours."

Anvin scowled.

"Are we not the same people?" he asked.

Leifall did not respond.

Anvin's face hardened.

"Our people need you," Anvin pressed. "Not here, behind your gates. But in the open field, where the battle is being fought."

Leifall shook his head.

"This is *your* war," he replied. "Is this not the revolution I have heard so much of, the one sparked by Duncan's daughter? The one who was playing with dragons?"

At the mention of his sister, Aidan felt a burning need to speak up, unable to quiet himself any longer.

"That is *my* sister you speak of," he called out, indignant, defensive. "And she only sparked the war that the rest of you were afraid to—the war that would stop us all from living as slaves, that would finally give us freedom."

Leifall scowled as he slowly turned to Aidan.

"Watch your tongue, boy. You're not so young that I won't put you in lashes."

Aidan stood his ground, feeling that this was his only chance to fight for his father.

"I will not," he said proudly, sticking out his chest. "I am Duncan's son. And I will tolerate no such speech of you. My father may be dying out there, and you are standing here, wasting time and words. Are you a warrior or not?"

Leifall's eyes widened in shock as he stared back at Aidan.

A long, tense silence followed, until finally, the commander took one step toward him.

"You are a fresh one, aren't you?" He stared Aidan down, and Aidan stood there, feeling a rush of nervousness. Slowly, the commander rubbed his beard. "Yet you stand up for your father. I like that," he said, surprising Aidan. "I wish my own sons were half as bold as you."

Aidan felt a rush of relief as the commander studied him. He felt that this was his chance to make his case and influence the destiny of his people.

"I asked my father to send me on this mission," Aidan replied, "because I thought you and your men would follow us, that you and your men were valorous. Does valor mean hiding behind a gate? Waiting for an enemy to come to you? Taking the safe route?"

Aidan took a deep breath, summoning all his courage, even though, deep inside, he was trembling.

"You can come and join my father in the greatest battle in history, in the greatest cause of your lives," Aidan said, "or you can stay here, hiding behind your gates, doing what boys do. Not what men do. Whatever you choose, I will leave this place and turn back and defend my father alone."

Leifall stared back for a long time, reddening, then finally shook his head.

"The better part of valor, boy, is knowing when to fight and where. Your father's tactics are foolish."

"My father freed all of Escalon before the Pandesians invaded."

"And where is he now? Asking for our help!"

"He asks for no man's help!" Aidan retorted indignantly. "He is offering you a *gift.*"

Leifall scoffed.

"A gift!"

His men laughed.

"And what gift is that?"

Aidan held his ground.

"The gift of valor," he replied.

Leifall studied Aidan for a long time, and Aidan stood there, feeling his heart pounding, knowing his father's destiny lay in these moments, trying to hold onto a brave face.

Finally, Leifall smiled.

"I like you, boy," he said. "I don't like your father, or his cause. But the blood in your veins runs true. You are right: we may be safer here. But safety is not what men were born for."

Leifall turned and nodded to his men, and suddenly a series of horns blew. Aidan looked up and saw dozens of warriors on the battlements stepping forward, all sounding horns, echoing each other, until finally, the gates opened.

There came a rumble, and moments later, there emerged hundreds of horses, riding fearlessly out for battle. As Aidan watched them all come, he felt his heart leap in anticipation. In victory.

"Let us go to your father, boy," Leifall said, laying a hand on his shoulder. "And let us show these Pandesians who the men of Escalon are."

CHAPTER TWENTY THREE

Duncan ran proudly, facing off against the battalions of Pandesian soldiers, clutching his sword and bracing himself for battle. Beside him stood a dozen soldiers, Kavos, Bramthos, and Seavig amongst them, all bravely making a stand with him against the incoming army. Duncan knew it would be a massacre. Yet his being here, making a stand, would also give the bulk of his forces the precious time they needed to retreat to the canyon. Saving his men was more important to Duncan than saving his own life.

Duncan also knew that they could not stand and wait here for the army to come to them. If they were going to die, they were going to do it bravely, boldly. Duncan charged with his men, all rushing forth boldly to meet the army. He felt emboldened having these fearless warriors by his side, all running in step with him, none hesitating to meet death in the face.

He had a plan, though. He was not ready to sacrifice their lives that quickly.

"CLOSE THE RANKS!" he commanded.

These veteran warriors all followed his command, coming shoulder to shoulder, tighter and tighter, a solid wall of men in step, charging like an arrowhead into the great army. Duncan looked up and saw the Pandesians hardly fifty feet away, on horses, rumbling right for them in a great cloud of dust.

Duncan waited and waited, his heart slamming, knowing they had to be disciplined, to wait until they got closer.

"RAISE THE SHIELDS!" he yelled, his command barely audible over the sound of the army.

His men huddled together in a tight semicircle and as one, raised their shields.

"PREPARE TO DEFEND!"

His men stopped and knelt together, as one.

The army hit them like a stampede, a wave of men and horses. As it did, Duncan felt himself reeling from the stampede of a million men and horses.

But they held the line. A solid wall of brass, they were able to block the incoming blows of hundreds of Pandesian soldiers. Horses stumbled and fell all around them, while dozens of soldiers fell head over heels, collapsing to the ground and causing an avalanche of fallen soldiers. Chaos and confusion spread quickly in the Pandesian ranks.

Duncan and his men held tight, despite the force of blows, all one unit, one wall of steel, preventing any swords or spears from getting through. Duncan waited for his moment of opportunity, and then he shouted:

"SWORDS!"

As one, the men quickly lowered their shields and stepped forward, stabbing the soldiers all around them. Duncan thrust his sword to the hilt in a soldier's stomach, watching as his eyes widened in shock.

Immediately, they all pulled back and raised the shields again, forming another wall of steel before the next wave of attacks came.

Again the blows rained down, and again they blocked them in every direction. Duncan's arms shook as he was slammed, feeling the pounding of battleaxes and halberds smashing against his shield, the sound of reverberating metal deafening in his ears.

"SWORDS!" Duncan boomed.

Again they lowered their shields and stabbed the soldiers before them.

Again and again Duncan used this maneuver, keeping his men safe against the much bigger army, while dropping dozens of Pandesians at a time. They were like an arrowhead cutting its way down the center of the army, creating great havoc while managing to stay alive.

Yet the storm of blows never paused, and Duncan felt as if he were up against the weight of the world. He blocked and stabbed, again and again, his face dripping with sweat and other men's blood. Soon enough, exhaustion crept in, his shoulders lowering just a bit. He breathed heavily in the stifling heat of the shield wall, and he knew he couldn't make this last forever. He could see his men tiring, too.

On the next wave, Duncan raised his shield just a bit too slowly, and a blow scraped his arm; he cried out in pain as he felt it tear flesh.

"SPEARS!" came a great cry, cutting through the air.

Duncan was immediately alert as he recognized it as the voice of the Supreme Ra.

He peeked out and saw Ra sitting on a horse with a golden harness, towering over all his men, at the rear of the army. No sooner had he uttered the command than dozens of spears soared through the air, sailing right for Duncan's men.

Duncan tightened his grip on his shield, raising it a bit higher to block, as did the others. A spear fell on his shield, bruising his arm, echoing in his ear with the clang. Yet his shield held.

Another spear fell, and another, dozens raining down, until soon his shield grew heavy with all the spears stuck to it. The shield crept lower and lower, until finally he lowered it and sliced off the spears. As he did, it left him exposed, and Duncan dropped to one knee, gasping in pain, as a spear grazed his shoulder. He heard a cry and watched Kavos's calf get grazed by a spear, too.

"ARCHERS!" cried Ra.

Duncan saw the Pandesians around them moving out of the way, and he saw in the distance a legion of archers step forward and prepare their bows.

Duncan's heart fell. He knew they could not survive this wave of arrows. They had made a brave stand and had gotten farther than he had ever expected, killing hundreds of men around them. But now they had reached the end of their run. If they were going to die, he figured, better to die not cowering behind a shield, but taking out as many men as they could in one last, valiant charge.

"MACES!" Duncan cried.

As one, his men all threw their shields, using them as weapons. Duncan bashed one soldier in the jaw, then used his shield as a disc, throwing it, severing the heads of several soldiers as it spun through the air with its sharpened edges. Duncan immediately drew his mace and raced forward into the throng with all his men.

They swung in wide circles, his men spacing out, creating distance from each other as they swung wider and wider. They struck and killed unsuspecting soldiers in a greater and greater circle, the air filling with the steel clang of spiked metal balls hitting armor, of armor rattling as Pandesians dropped in all directions. The circle grew wider and wider, till they had created a perimeter of fifty feet right in the center of the army, none of the Pandesians able to get close to them.

At the same time, the archers came forward. They leaned back and raised their bows to the sky, and as they did, Duncan braced himself, knowing he was about to die.

But then, suddenly, everyone froze. There came an eerie silence in the battle, as all the soldiers, on both sides, looked up to the sky up in terror. Duncan, baffled, looked up, too—and was stunned by what he saw.

There came a roar as the skies parted, and Duncan's heart quickened as he saw who it was. Theon. He had come for them. Theon, Duncan was elated to see, dove down right for the Pandesian soldiers, opened his mouth wide, and breathed fire.

Shrieks filled the air as one row after another of Pandesian soldiers were aflame, starting with the archers. Within moments, the flames rippled through the ranks, and thousands of Pandesian soldiers lay dead, Theon creating a wide perimeter around Duncan and his men.

As Duncan watched, riveted, in awe at the dragon's power, Theon finally swooped down and breathed a huge wall of flame, separating Duncan from the rest of the army—and giving Duncan and his men the precious time they needed to retreat.

"To the canyon!" Duncan cried.

His men all fell in beside him and they ran, as one, away from the Pandesians, away from the wall of fire, and to the distant canyon. It was there, Duncan knew, that he would make his last stand. He had achieved his goal: the bulk of his men were free, safe, in the canyon. Now it was time for him to join them, and to have one last chance to fight the Pandesians on his own terms.

As Duncan and his men sprinted from the flaming battlefield for the canyon, perhaps still a hundred yards away, heaving for air, behind him, he could hear Theon's flames begin to dry up. He heard the baby dragon flying away, and he knew his fire had run out. His time was limited before Ra's army caught up.

Duncan, heart pounding, redoubled his speed. He saw the edge of the canyon getting closer, and he wondered how his men had done on their surprise assault on Baris. He prayed they had been successful.

Yet Duncan's heart dropped when he neared and heard the triumphant shouts of men—not his own—and he knew all was not well. As he reached the edge, he and his men stopped short and gazed down below. He saw the bulk of his men fighting bravely on the steep slope of the canyon walls—and not doing well. He saw the dozens of dead bodies, saw his men surrounded on all sides, falling by the minute, and he realized Baris had somehow anticipated their coming and led them into a trap. Duncan's men were stuck, trapped on a broad plateau, fighting Baris's men below—and yet somehow also flanked by Baris's men above. Duncan looked closely and saw that Bant had taken advantage of secret stone passages, small tunnels in the canyon, and even now had hundreds of his men pouring out of them, above Duncan's men, attacking them from both sides.

His men, clearly not anticipating this, were falling by the dozens as they tried unsuccessfully to fight on two fronts at once. Duncan watched in horror and indignation as several dropped, shrieking, spears hurled into their backs. Bant's treachery and deceit never ceased to amaze him.

Duncan tightened his grip on his sword, breathing hard with fury, and felt his destiny rise up within him. He sensed that he, with but a dozen men, could defeat hundreds and free his men, if he caught them by surprise, used the high ground, and with speed and valor at his back.

"CHARGE!" he commanded.

The dozen fearless warriors beside him were already at a sprint, all racing down the steep slope, stumbling and not caring as they zeroed in on Bant's men below. They sprinted straight down the canyon, Duncan's heart pounding in his ears.

As he neared, Bant's men turned and looked up over their shoulders at the commotion—and were clearly shocked to find themselves outflanked, too. Duncan, seeing a soldier about to stab one of his men in the back, knew there was no time. He raised his sword and threw it, and watched it turn end over end and then find a place in a soldier's back, felling him, and saving Duncan's man.

Duncan did not hesitate. He threw himself into the mob, drawing the other sword on his belt, swinging two swords at once, chopping off the heads of three soldiers before any could even raise a shield. He felt his veins, his entire being, burning for vengeance against Bant and his people, and determined to free his men.

108

His dozen soldiers were as determined as he, Kavos, Bramthos and Seavig throwing themselves into battle, hacking down dozens of men, felling them and causing an immediate panic in the group.

They fought their way straight down the mountain face, cutting through the lines, forcing Bant's men to retreat back down the slope. As they did, they retreated into the arms of the rest of Duncan's forces, led by Arthfael, who immediately hacked them down. Sandwiched from both sides, collapsing in panic, Bant's force of soldiers at the canyon top were soon all dead. Many were killed on the spot, while others Duncan and his men hurled down the mountain face, their tumbling bodies like boulders, taking out more men below.

Duncan was soon reunited with his men, and they all let out a cheer, one solidified force, holding the high ground. Now they all turned and looked down below, and knew they had only to contend with Bant's army below.

"CHARGE!" Duncan cried.

They all charged down the canyon slope together, regaining momentum as they fought back against Bant's stunned and retreating men. Bant's men, caught off guard, could not retreat fast enough, and Duncan felled them left and right. Duncan felt a mounting optimism, and he felt that soon the canyon could actually be theirs. A thousand soldiers awaited them below, but now they had the momentum and the high ground.

Duncan led his men, hacking through soldiers as they fought their way down to a broad plateau near the canyon bottom. From here, it was but a hundred feet to the canyon floor, to vanquishing the rest of Bant's army, and to victory.

As Duncan rallied with all his men, preparing for the final advance, suddenly, he felt the ground shake beneath him. He looked down, baffled. He looked over and narrowed his eyes as he saw Bant's men chopping massive ropes. A rumbling followed, and Duncan looked up to see a massive boulder swing on a rope. He braced himself, too late, as a moment later it smashed into the underside of the plateau on which he stood.

There came an awful cracking noise, the sound of rock splitting, and Duncan looked down with horror to see the plateau he stood on separating from the canyon wall. His world turned sideways, he was thrown off balance, and suddenly he and all his men were falling through the air, tumbling in an avalanche of rubble, hurtling down to the army below, and to an instant and sure death.

CHAPTER TWENTY FOUR

Dierdre stood in the rubble of the Tower of Ur, Marco beside her, each bracing themselves as the nation of trolls burst through the woods and charged right for them. Dierdre could not fathom how so many trolls could be in Escalon, how they could have all burst through the Flames. It did not seem possible. Unless, she realized with dread, the Flames had fallen.

If that were the case, then Escalon was finished. A country without borders was no country at all. Without the Flames, Escalon would be nothing but the playground of the savage Marda. Dierdre knew in that terrible moment that not only was *her* life over, but that all of Escalon would be destroyed. She was wracked with pain at the thought. What a terrible way for this beautiful land to end, she thought, its great coastal cities flooded by Pandesian fleets, its great northern plains overrun by trolls, burning their way south. It was a land destroyed by fire and water, ravaged from both ends.

Dierdre stood there and braced herself, the northernmost victim of this terrible plague of trolls, prepared to die with the rest of her country. She squeezed Marco's hand, the two of them able to do nothing but stand there and die. As Dierdre looked death in the face, she no longer missed her father; on the contrary, she was relieved that she would soon join him. She did, though, feel filled with regret that she would never see Kyra again, never know what had happened to her, and that she would not have a chance to avenge her father's death.

As the trolls neared, halberds raised, Dierdre saw the sharpened blades coming down right for her chest and she anticipated the feeling of pain. She closed her eyes, preparing for the worst.

Yet moments later, Dierdre opened her eyes and was in shock not to feel anything, not to feel steel entering her flesh, or to feel herself being stampeded by trolls. Instead, she heard a clang, the sound of metal on metal.

Dierdre looked up and saw a halberd bouncing harmlessly off an invisible shield, inches away from her face. She watched, baffled, as the trolls all charged and smashed into this same invisible wall, stopping in their tracks, stumbling and falling all around her and stampeding each other. It was as if they had run into a wall.

She looked over and was amazed to see that Marco, beside her, also stood unharmed, as if he too were protected by this invisible shield. She then saw the army of trolls look past her, at the tower, in fear. She turned, too, and was amazed at what she saw.

There, emerging from the rubble, came a man, stepping up to the highest boulder. He was encircled by an aura of white light, shining in every direction. As Dierdre examined him, she was stunned to see that he resembled Kyra, in male form. He looked as if he could be her father.

Dierdre looked at his glowing yellow eyes and realized at once what he was: a Watcher. He stood there with a staff held high, and as he did, light radiated down from it to the nation of trolls below. The light encircled her and Marco, creating a bubble around them, sparing them from attack. The light then ripped through the crowd and smashed hundreds of trolls, sending them flying to the ground. It was like a wave of fire passing through.

Dierdre, wondering who this mysterious man was, forever grateful to him for saving her life, watched as he leapt down off the rubble and landed beside her.

"Stand back," he commanded, his voice ancient and firm.

She and Marco retreated as he stepped forward and fearlessly walked into the incoming mob of trolls. She watched in awe as he took on an army alone, swinging his staff, each blow sending sparks of light showering down as he smashed one troll in the ribs, jabbed another in the neck, slashed another in the chest. He swung his staff so fast it was a blur, around over his head, then behind his back, knocking out trolls in every direction in a shower of light.

A horrific shout cut through the air, and Dierdre turned to see thousands more trolls suddenly burst through the forest from all sides. The Watcher was soon surrounded on all sides. He swung his staff in a circle, smashing down the incoming trolls again and again, creating a wider and wider perimeter—and yet, too many trolls flooded the place. Dierdre saw him begin to tire.

The trolls pressed in on him from all sides, and clearly he had not expected such a flood—an entire nation. She saw him slipping, and she knew he could not last.

She could not let him die, and she knew Marco would not, either. At the same time, they each raised their sword and charged, running recklessly into the mob, swinging, fighting their way to save him. Protected by the bubble, they hacked down trolls on all sides of them, and soon, they found themselves at his side. All three of them were inside their shrinking bubble, surrounded, engulfed, the shields wearing off.

It was a valiant defense, but it was not enough.

In moments, she knew, they would be finished.

CHAPTER TWENTY FIVE

Aidan's heart pounded as his horse galloped across the barren landscape, Anvin beside him, White running at his feet, and all around them, the hundreds of warriors of Leptus, led by Leifall. Aidan felt the thrill of riding into battle, felt for the first time that he was one of the men, truly a warrior. Here he was, riding up front, preparing to meet the enemy, to save his father. He had been successful in his mission; thanks to him, the men of Leptus were riding to rescue his father.

The thought of what lay waiting for him just beyond the horizon, his father, stranded, needing reinforcements, made Aidan forget his fear. He thought single-mindedly of saving him, of proving to his father that he was the son he had raised him to be. And that quelled all his fears. They had been riding for hours since Leptus, and as they neared the canyon, Aidan heard a rumble in the distance, sounding like thunder. It was, he knew with a jolt, the sound of battle. Of men killing each other.

It rumbled and echoed, bouncing off what could only be the walls of the canyon, reverberating even from here—and as it did, Aidan felt a sense of desperation. He tried to suppress a feeling of panic as he tried not to imagine the awful things that could be happening to his father. Were they killing his people? Was he arriving too late?

Father, he urged silently, *wait for us. Hang in there, just a little bit longer.*

Aidan thought of all his father's men, trapped, thought of Cassandra, and even of Motley. He knew they were vastly outnumbered, and the idea of them all dying before he could reach them tore him up inside.

They crested a hill and the landscape opened before them and in the distance he could see the canyon. His fears compounded when he heard a crash and watched a huge ledge give away, saw the cloud of dust. He felt as if he were dying inside as he watched his father's men falling into the canyon, shrieking, crushing each other.

It was an awful sight. He could hear the agony of men dying even from here, and he felt a feeling of dread as he saw his life flash before him. He had, it seemed, been just a few minutes too late.

"FORWARD!" Anvin shrieked, kicking his horse, spurring the other men into action.

The men of Leptus rode hard, keeping up with him, and Aidan joined, too, his legs chafed from the horse, his palms burning from gripping the reins. Breathing hard, he lowered his head and kicked even harder, determined not to let his father die.

They closed in on the canyon and finally reached its perimeter, all of them coming to a sudden stop at the edge, before falling over. Aidan looked down, and his heart broke. There, below, were hundreds of his father's men, sprawled out in unnatural positions, crushed on the canyon floor.

Dead.

Yet Aidan's heart leapt with hope as he saw a small contingent of his father's men had survived the fall, were fighting for their lives, down far below on the canyon floor—and then his heart soared to see his father down there amongst them, fighting with a small group of warriors. They were injured, covered in dirt and dust, their back against a pile of rubble. Yet still, they were alive.

Aidan saw his father fighting furiously in all directions, surrounded. They were a crippled force, caught off guard by the collapse of the canyon shelf, and now surrounded by the enemy. They clearly had but moments until they were completely wiped out.

Anvin was already kicking his horse, galloping for the edge of the canyon, taking the steep slope heading down. Aidan followed with the others, and as he neared, he was shocked to see how steep it was. He looked straight down, and it seemed to be an impossible descent.

Yet he watched in awe as Anvin rode straight down the slope, somehow managing to hang on, somehow, amazingly, his horse keeping its footing. Eventually, near the bottom, Anvin straightened as the canyon leveled out.

Inspired, Aidan followed him, joining all the men of Leptus. His heart pounded in terror as he held his breath and tried not to look. He rode straight down and felt his stomach dropping in his throat at the plunge. He wrapped his arms tight around the mane and was sure he was going to die. He felt at any moment he would fall straight over the horse's head and be crushed. The angle was too steep.

Yet he thought of his father down there and forced himself to hang on. He felt paralyzed with fear, and tried not to imagine his death, lost in a cloud of dust and men.

Around him, he heard shouts, and he watched as some of the horses lost their footing, the angle too steep. They stumbled and fell, tumbling head over heels straight down the mountain and for their deaths. More than a few of the men following them tripped over them, and died, too.

Aidan held on, feeling as if he were riding straight down, praying this hell would end, that he would not end up like those men. He squeezed his eyes shut and did not expect to reopen them.

Finally, Aidan felt his stomach correct, his breathing return to normal, and he opened his eyes and was amazed to see the terrain had leveled off. He looked out, and was stunned that he had made it to the canyon's bottom. He felt overcome with joy, with victory. He had conquered his fear.

Aidan looked around and saw that most of the others had made it, too, and Leptus' army, hundreds of men, shouted out in victory, all of them racing across the canyon floor, sounding horns, and heading for his father.

Bant's men, fighting his father, all stopped at the sound and turned and watched them come, surprise and fear in their faces. For the first time, they had been caught off guard themselves, outflanked in their own territory.

Aidan spotted his father fighting off three men in the distance; he saw Kavos, Seavig and Bramthos swinging flails in circles to keep men at bay, and saw Motley holding a shield and Cassandra a staff and jabbing soldiers who got too close. They were just barely fending men off who, with every passing moment, pressed in closer all around them.

Aidan, inspired by the sight, charged, throwing himself into the fray, Anvin and White by his side, not even thinking of the consequences.

White reached them first. He leapt into the air and sank his teeth into the throat of a soldier who was about to stab Motley. The soldier fell to the ground, shrieking, and Motley lowered his shield in surprise and relief.

At the same time, Aidan raised his sword and did not even think twice as he charged for a soldier who was facing off against

Cassandra. The man had just managed to knock the spear from her hand, and he was about to stab her. Aidan, realizing he wouldn't reach him in time, raised his sword and threw it.

It tumbled end over end, and to his shock, actually lodged itself in the soldier's back, killing him. The man collapsed to the ground, face-first, at Cassandra's feet.

Aidan felt numb. It was the first time he had ever killed a man, a real, living human being, and while he was thrilled to save Cassandra, he felt nauseated. It was a surreal feeling to take another's life, one of both victory and sadness.

Cassandra looked back at him, love and admiration in her eyes, a look he had never seen before. It was a look that made all of this worth it. It emboldened him. Cassandra, seeing him defenseless, reached down, grabbed a flail from the ground, and threw it to him, and he snatched it happily in mid-air by the hilt.

With White running to Cassandra and Motley's side to help keep them safe, Aidan felt free to ride off into the crowd, spotting his father. He found him across the canyon, fighting off three men at once, alternately raising his shield and slashing with his sword, the clanging ringing out as swords slashed down on his shield and armor. His father looked injured, weakened, and losing strength by the moment.

Hang on, Father, Aidan urged.

Anvin rode up beside him, clearly having the same idea, and the two of them rode, bursting through the crowd of soldiers, ignoring the fighting all around them and determined only to reach Duncan in time. Aidan swung his flail furiously, blindly. It clanged as he rode, smashing into the armor, shields, knocking swords from soldiers' hands. He did not know how many men he had injured or disarmed, and he did not stop to check.

Beside him, Anvin expertly slashed soldiers left and right, parrying blows and dropping them. They hacked their way through the mob, while all around them the crowd of Bant's soldiers began to thin, fighting off attacks from Leptus' men on all sides, the fighting now bloody and hand-to-hand. Aidan, thinking of his father, forced his way through the thick crowd, narrowly dodging the blow of a hatchet, seeing his father trapped behind a pile of rubble from where the cliff had collapsed and knowing he had to get to him soon.

Aidan was finally able to peer through the dust, and his heart quickened to see his father facing off with Bant, the two of them surrounded by Bant's men. Clearly, the pivotal fight of the war was taking place.

Duncan fought valiantly, he and Bant slashing and parrying, swords clanging off of shields, driving each other back and forth, neither he nor Bant able to gain an inch—yet Aidan could see Bant's other men closing in, tightening the circle, and he knew his father could be betrayed and die at any moment. He kicked his horse with all he had, and with one last sprint across the canyon, he closed the gap. He swung his flail with blind passion with one hand, barely hanging onto the reins with the other, closing in—when he found himself abruptly blocked by a dozen of Bant's men.

Aidan's horse slowed when suddenly Anvin came charging beside him, taking on the group. Aidan found an opening, saw his chance, and burst through the narrow gap, breaking through the circle to reach his father.

Aidan rode all the way, bracing himself for a deadly blow as soldiers swung at him and barely missed, until finally, to his own surprise, he managed to reach the circle of Bant's men surrounding his father. He did not know what he would do when he got there—he just wanted to create a distraction and give his father a chance.

Aidan burst into the stunned group, his horse trampling men as he charged them from behind. A few fell, while others turned to see what the commotion was. Aidan raised the flail and swung and threw it blindly into the group of men, realizing he had to create a distraction, and men raised their hands to their faces, distracted, while the long chain and spiked ball knocked the weapons from several of their hands.

But Aidan suddenly felt a horrible pain in his side, heard a loud clang in his ears, and realized he had been smashed by a club and a shield. He fell from his horse down to the ground, the pain of hitting the ground worse than the blow. On the ground, weaponless, the other men closed in on him.

There suddenly came a shout, and Aidan looked up through the group to see his father get a second wind, clearly energized by the sight of his son. Having the distraction he needed, his father charged mercilessly into the group of soldiers, hacking three of them down without even slowing. As he did, his father's men rallied around him, all pouncing on the soldiers, who, caught off guard, panicked and tried to flee.

Aidan turned to see a soldier raise a hatchet for him, and he knew he would not have time to react. He braced himself for death.

Suddenly, the man gasped, and Aidan saw his father standing behind him, his sword run through the man's back, while the man dropped down, dead.

Aidan felt his father's beefy palm grabbing his chest, quickly dragging him to his feet. His father embraced him tight, as all around his men fought back, dropping Bant's men, the momentum now in their favor. Aidan's father held Aidan's head to his chest, clearly brimming with pride.

And Aidan, too, for the first time felt himself relax, fill with pride. He had done it. He had saved his father.

Now the tides were turning, as all around them the battle raged on. Aidan felt himself shoved and he turned to see his father push him out of harm's way, as a soldier stepped out of the crowd and faced off with him.

Bant.

Duncan drew his sword and stepped forward, while a circle of soldiers from both armies formed around the men as they faced off man-to-man in its last, pivotal battle.

"You should've stayed in Andros," Bant snarled to Duncan. "It would have been a quicker death."

"For you, maybe," Duncan replied.

The circle grew thicker as more and more men stopped to watch the decisive battle, the two men circling each other warily, each waiting for his chance to strike.

"I will kill you as I did your sons!" Bant cried.

"And I will avenge the cowardly way you killed them," Duncan retorted.

They let out a battle cry and each charged like two old rams, neither slowing, each clearly unwilling to stop until they killed the other.

Duncan raised his sword, Bant his hatchet, and there came a terrible clang as their weapons locked. They stood there, each grunting, neither able to get the best of the other.

Finally, Duncan kicked Bant in the chest, sending him stumbling back and down to his back in the dirt. He then rushed forward and kicked, knocking the hatchet from his hand.

Bant rolled and tried to recover it, but Duncan stepped on his hand, then kicked him again, knocking him back.

Duncan leaned over to pick him up, but Bant sneakily grabbed a handful of dirt and spun and threw it at Duncan's eyes.

Aidan's heart leapt as he saw his father blinded. Duncan stumbled back, and Bant, taking advantage, jumped to his feet and kicked him, sending him stumbling to the ground, dropping his sword.

Duncan lay there, defenseless, and Aidan went instinctively to rush forward, to help his father—but suddenly a strong hand on his chest held him back. He looked up to see Anvin standing there, shaking his head, warning him not to interfere between the solo combat.

Bant rushed forward, about to stomp Duncan in the face, but Duncan rolled out of the way at the final moment. In the same motion, Aidan was proud to see, Duncan raised his foot and swept it around and kicked Bant behind the knee, dropping him.

Duncan then grabbed his sword, wiped the sand from his eyes, and smashed Bant in the back of the neck with the hilt, sending him down face first in the dirt.

Duncan stood, breathing hard, wiping blood from his mouth, and looked down at Bant in disgust. He reached down, grabbed the limp Bant, and held him from behind, a dagger to his throat.

Silence fell amongst both armies, all the soldiers crowded around, all eyes to them.

"Tell your men to lay down their arms," Duncan growled to Bant.

Bant shook his head, spitting up blood.

"Never," Bant replied. "You can kill us all, but it won't help you. You will soon die with us. The Pandesians will kill you all anyway."

Duncan sneered.

"For my sons," he said with contempt, and in that same motion, he sliced Bant's throat.

Aidan watched, shocked, as the leader of Baris slumped down to the ground, dead.

All of Bant's men seemed to have the life taken out of them as they watched their leader die, and as one, they all dropped their weapons and raised their hands.

There arose a loud cheer, and Aidan finally breathed easy, as the men crowded around his father, victorious. The canyon was theirs.

*

Duncan stood in the canyon, surrounded by Leifall, Anvin, Kavos, Bramthos, Arthfael, Seavig, Aidan and his hundreds of men, all survivors of the brutal battle. All around them the canyon floor was littered, amidst the rubble, with the corpses of hundreds of soldiers, some Duncan's men and others Bant's. There was a sense of victory in the air, yet it was also a somber one.

Duncan embraced Anvin, who embraced him back, overflowing with gratitude for his men's loyalty and bravery. One at a time, he clasped men's shoulders, finally reaching Leptus and his men, so grateful and proud of each of them.

"I owe you a great debt of gratitude, my friend," Duncan said to Anvin, "for convincing these men to come to our aid."

"It is your son you must thank," Anvin corrected.

Duncan turned to Aidan, standing there amongst his men, and looked at him with surprise.

"Aidan convinced these men to join our cause," Anvin continued. "Without him, I doubt they'd be here."

Duncan walked over to his son and squeezed his shoulder, more proud of him than he could say.

"You are no longer a boy," he said to Aidan, "you are a man among men."

Duncan's men cheered in response, and Duncan was elated to see Aidan look back up at him with so much pride.

Duncan looked over and saw Motley standing by his side.

"And you, Motley," Duncan said, clasping his arm. "You took a great chance to save a stranger."

Motley beamed back, clearly not used to being thanked by a soldier.

Duncan turned and surveyed the canyon floor, saw all of his men, saw the survivors combing the battlefield, climbing over corpses, scavenging for weapons, regrouping. He saw all of Bant's men, all prisoners now, all staring back, all awaiting their fates. He turned and faced them, growing somber. He knew that a good commander should execute all these men, to protect his flank.

"You are all warriors," he called out to them, as they stared back anxiously, "men of Escalon, just as we. The blood of our forefathers runs through you, as it does through us. We are one people and one nation. Your mistake was joining the cause of a traitor. But that does not make you traitors yourselves. Sometimes good men, out of misguided loyalty, serve bad commanders."

He sighed, surveying them all, as they stared back hopefully.

"So I shall give you all one more chance," he said. "In these times we need every man we can get. You can die by our swords, or you can renounce your former commander, the dead traitor Bant, and join ranks with my men. Which will it be?" he asked.

A thick silence fell, as all his men crowded close to watch.

The lead soldier among Bant's several hundred men stepped forward, his hands in shackles, and stared back solemnly.

"You are a good man," he replied, "and a fine commander. Bant was wrong to betray you, and we were wrong to follow him. No other commander would have spared us. That alone makes our decision easy. We are with you! Let us fight together, as one, and kill these dogs who have invaded Escalon!"

"WE ARE WITH YOU!" all of Bant's men cried.

Duncan's heart lifted with optimism and relief. He nodded to his men, and they all stepped forward and broke the shackles binding Bant's men, freeing them, all.

Duncan turned and surveyed the army, now one, their ranks bolstered, and he wondered: where to go from here? They had avenged themselves against Bant. They had regrouped. They were stronger than ever. Yet still, they could not attack Andros, not with the dragons there, and not with the Pandesians there in force.

Duncan turned to the rest of his men, and slowly, he grew serious.

"MEN!" he called out. "Here we stand, at the base of the canyon, alive, but the Pandesians will arrive here soon enough. We will be trapped here in this hole in the earth, stuck in the low ground."

He looked them all over.

"You have all fought valiantly, and we have lost many good brothers on the field of battle today," he continued. "Bant is dead, and we have one less front to worry about. Yet the Pandesians await us, and we cannot meet them on their terms. The time has come to execute the next part of our plan."

A long silence fell over the men, all looking to him with eager eyes.

"The time has come to lure them to this canyon—and to flood it."

The men all stared back, fear in their faces, unsure. The silence grew thick and tense.

Duncan turned to Leifall, the commander of Leptus.

"Everfall," Duncan said. "It can be done, can it not?"

Leifall rubbed his beard, skeptical.

"The falls are strong, that is true," he replied. "Strong enough to create a river. That river, if redirected, could theoretically reach the canyon." Leifall shook his head. "But it's never been done."

"Yet it's possible," Duncan persisted.

Leifall shrugged.

"Everfall flows into the Bay of Death," he said. "You propose changing the course of nature. You would have to reroute the channels in the mountain face. There are levers, ancient levers from the dawn of time, for such a purpose, for a time of war. But they have, to my knowledge, never been used."

Leifall sighed, as a long silence fell over the men, all of them staring.

"A bold plan," he finally said. "Risky. Improbable."

"Yet possible?" Duncan asked.

Leifall rubbed his beard for a long time, then finally, he nodded.

"Anything is possible."

Duncan nodded. That was all he needed to her.

"I will lure the Pandesians into the canyon then," he called out to his men, emboldened, "and you and your men will redirect the falls here."

Leifall stared back, concerned.

"There is one thing you are not considering, Duncan," he added, with concern. "If this works, you will trap yourself, here, at

123

the base of the canyon, and be flooded with the Pandesians. You may drown, too."

Duncan nodded, having already considered that.

"Then that is a chance I will have to take."

CHAPTER TWENTY SIX

The Holy and Supreme Ra paced the stone battlements of the castle of Andros, furious. High above, the dragons still crisscrossed, raining down fire on the streets of the capital, shrieks filling the air as men burned alive in the street. Rumbles made the ground shake, as building after building was swiped by their great talons, knocked to the ground. This capital building, with its golden dome and walls of gold, seemed the only safe place left.

Worse, Ra had been forced, on the open battlefield, to retreat in humiliation. He had almost had Duncan in his grasp, until that dragon, Theon, had arrived and snatched away his victory. It was a humiliation he refused to accept.

Retreating back to the capital had been the only thing he could do at that time. Theon could not pursue them here, not to Andros, with all these other dragons. It had given Ra a chance to regroup his men, at least for now, though coming here, back into the dragons' den, had made him lose many more.

Night was mercifully falling now, though, and he would be able to use that to his advantage. Ra could march his men at night, in total blackness, out of sight of the dragons, back after Duncan. They would march swiftly back to the canyon, and kill Duncan at the crack of dawn while he and his men still slept. The Great Ra never forgot a vendetta.

Yet still, Ra was not satisfied with one mere plan of victory. Like all great commanders, he needed a backup plan. A plan not only of brawn, yet also one of trickery. Something to assure that this time, no matter what happened, Duncan would die. Yet what that backup plan should be, he still did not know.

Ra looked out at his chamber, packed with advisors and counselors and generals and sorcerers, all of them cowering in fear from the dragons' breath outside, all of them debating his course of action. Tired of mulling over his own thoughts, he nodded to his men.

"You may speak now," he finally said to his general, who had been kneeling before him, waiting to speak for hours.

"My Most Holy and Supreme Ra," the general began, his voice tremulous with fear. "I bring the report you asked for. The dragons did more damage than we expected. We have lost nearly half of our men to their flames, not only here, in Andros, but also in the rest of Escalon. And many more of our men who were spared from the dragons' breath have been killed by the legions of trolls flooding in from the north. We need to urgently stop the tide of trolls, and we need to find a way to defend against the rise of the dragons."

Ra clenched his jaw in rage, listening impatiently.

"We waste our resources chasing Duncan in the south," the commander continued. "We need to take the battle to the north. We need to find a way to restore the Flames and to stop the trolls from flooding the border. Otherwise, we cannot win this war on so many fronts."

The chamber fell silent, all eyes to Ra.

Ra nodded, and slowly rose from his throne. He descended, taking a few steps toward the general.

"Rise, General," he said, laying a hand on his shoulder.

The general rose and looked up at him with hope, and fear.

"I thank you for your report," Ra added.

The general smiled, looking relieved.

"And I thank you for your opinion," Ra added.

In the same breath, without warning, he suddenly stabbed the general in the heart.

The general, shocked, dropped to the ground, dead, and all the other generals stared back at Ra, filled with dread.

Ra breathed, filled with fury. He hated compromise. He hated being told what he could not do. And he hated weakness.

What was it about Escalon? he fumed, wondering. Was it cursed? In every other place in the world, he had been able to conquer and hold it. But in this land, problems arose from every corner.

He turned to one of his other generals.

"And what would *you* suggest?" he asked.

The other general gulped, looking back nervously.

"If you were to ask me, my Most Holy and Awesome Lord," he replied, tentative, "we should retreat. Abandon this land. Let the trolls destroy it. Let the dragons destroy it. And then let the dragons destroy the trolls. Let them all kill each other. Most of Escalon's men are dead or enslaved anyway. Our business is done here. And years from now, when the dragons have left and the trolls are dead, we can come back and inhabit it—without losing any more men."

Ra trembled with anger.

"Retreat?" he asked, indignant. "Come here," he added.

The general gulped in terror as Ra walked him to the stone balcony.

"My Holy and Awesome Lord," he began. "I meant you no disrespect—"

Before he could finish speaking, Ra reached out, grabbed him, and threw him over the balcony.

The general shrieked as he plummeted and fell face first on the ground below, dead.

Ra stood on the stone balcony, seething, staring out as a dragon swooped down and picked up the corpse and ate it.

Finally, Ra turned back inside and looked back at the other men in his chamber. They all looked away, terrified to meet his gaze. He breathed, debating.

Finally, he stepped forward.

"We will pursue Duncan and his men with all of our power," he finally boomed. "After his capture and torture, you will burn his men alive, along with any trace of what was once left of Escalon. Now go. Invade the canyon. And do not return to me without his head."

The men all turned and rushed from the room, leaving Ra alone in the chamber. Only one remained behind. Khtha. His sorcerer. He stood there alone, in the center of the empty chamber, staring back with glowing red eyes, obscured by his cloak and hood.

Ra stared back, intrigued.

"What do you see?" Ra asked, almost afraid to know the answer. Khtha always had an uncanny ability to see into the future.

"It is… obscured, for now," he began, his voice gravelly, unhuman. "Yet I see…a great battle of forces….Yet who shall win…remains unwritten."

"Then what good are you to me?" Ra snapped, infuriated. "Leave me at once."

Ra turned his back on him, but Khtha called out:

"I have a plan for you."

Ra slowly turned back, his interest piqued.

"Go on," he commanded.

"I can change your visage," Khtha said. "Transform your outward appearance."

Ra furrowed his brow, intrigued.

"And who shall I become?" Ra asked.

There followed a long silence, until finally Khtha replied:

"Kyra."

Ra felt the hairs on his arms stand on end, sensing immediately that the plan was the right one.

"You can infiltrate their lines," Khtha continued. "They will trust you, Kyra. You will get face to face with Duncan. And you, his daughter, can put the knife in his heart directly."

Khtha, for the first time, grinned, a grotesque, evil grin.

Ra could not help grinning back. This was the exact backup plan he needed, if his armies should fail.

He nodded.

Khtha stepped forward and slowly raised a trembling hand, pale, shriveled, and as Ra closed his eyes, he felt the sorcerer's hand reach up and cover his face, felt the slimy fingertips cover his eyelids.

Slowly, Ra felt himself transforming. He felt his body changing, his hair growing longer, his face becoming smooth. It burned, and it felt as if it were eating him up alive. He shrieked in agony.

Yet, finally, it was done.

Khtha, finished, held up a looking glass. Ra took it, breathless, and his heart stopped as he saw who was looking back at him:

Kyra.

Ra grinned and laughed a deep, evil laugh, yet somehow it sounded just like her.

"Father," he said, his voice hers, "I am coming for you."

CHAPTER TWENTY SEVEN

Merk braced himself as he stood on the edge of the isle of Knossos and looked up in horror at the flock of dragons diving down right for him. Waves from the Bay of Death crashed at his feet, men were dying all around him from the trolls' invasion, and behind him Lorna and her scores of Watchers summoned these ancient creatures to their rescue. Whether these dragons would rescue them or kill them was unclear—and now it seemed they were out of her control.

A terrible roar shook the air as scores of dragons dove for the waters, talons extended, their terrible teeth showing as they opened their jaws wide. Merk glanced back to the fort and saw the Watchers leaning out the windows, palms raised to the sky, while Lorna stood before them, light radiating from their palms up into the clouds. He looked down at the thousands of trolls covering the rocky cliffs of Knossos, overpowering the warriors—indeed, a group of them rushed for him even now. It was a dire scene for the men of Knossos.

Yet, in a moment, everything changed. The dragons swooped down and, with their long talons, targeted the trolls, slicing them to pieces before they could reach him.

Awful cries rang out as body parts went flying, the long claws cutting through the trolls like butter, sending them falling off the rock, down to the sea. Some of the dragons grabbed the trolls—two, three, four at a time—carried them up into the skies and dropped them down into the rocks, watching them splat. Other dragons scooped up trolls and ate them alive.

The dragons circled around again, and this time, they pulled back their wings, opened their great mouths, and a terrible hissing noise followed as they breathed down a wall of flame.

Merk braced himself, taking cover behind his shield, feeling the heat even from here, as the dragons took aim at the thousands of trolls still covering the cliffs. The trolls' cries of agony rose even above the sound of the flames. Those who weren't lucky enough to be killed on the spot turned and jumped off the cliffs, preferring a death by water than one by fire.

Some trolls, though, survived, and these, still on fire, raced for cover on the isle of Knossos. A few ran for Merk, aflame, desperate, following a primal instinct of survival, not ready to jump over the edge. It appeared to be a death charge; they clearly wanted to grab Merk, and the other soldiers, and set them aflame, too. Misery wanted company.

Merk braced himself. He was not prepared to die, and certainly not this way.

As they neared, he leaned back and kicked back the trolls, his boot catching fire, then leaned forward and stabbed them through the chest. He kicked at them again and again, keeping them at bay, then finally stamped out the fire on his foot. Other trolls he smashed with his shield, fighting frantically to keep them away and keep himself from catching fire.

Merk heard cries all around him and looked over to see that some of the other warriors of Knossos were not so lucky. A troll, aflame, managing to grab one, squeezed him in a hug, and carried him with him as he leapt over the edge into the water. Their shrieks could be heard even out of sight, a terrible sound that made Merk want to forget it.

Merk saw their leader, Vesuvius, on the isle of Knossos, encircled by flames, look over the cliffs, desperate, clearly afraid to fall. He opportunistically grabbed two of his trolls and in one quick motion, shoved them over the edge. He jumped over with them.

Merk rushed to the edge and watched as they all fell. Vesuvius spun his trolls around in the air and used them as cushions, making sure to land atop them, breaking his fall with their bodies as they landed in the waters. His trolls were dead, crushed beneath his weight, but Vesuvius swam away, untouched. Merk could hardly believe what a cruel and heartless leader he was, as easily prepared to kill his own men as he was the enemy. A formidable foe, Merk realized, one without any morals.

The dragons circled wider, broadening their reach, and dove for the water. They dove down close, fearless, the trolls' spears merely bouncing off their hardened scales. They set the troll ships aflame, fire meeting water in a great hiss of steam.

It was a chaotic, brutal scene. One chaos had been replaced with another.

As the ranks of trolls attacking the island thinned, Merk saw a look of horror spread across Lorna's face. Despite the intense flashes of light emanating from their palms, the dragons, done with the trolls, turned and, with blood in their eyes, set their sights back on the isle of Knossos. Merk felt a sense of dread as he realized they had lost control of the dragons.

"Take cover!" Merk called out.

It was too late. The dragons opened their mouths, flew at them impossibly fast, and a moment later a wall of flame slowly filled the ocean, creating a wall of steam, hissing, spreading right for the isle of Knossos. It wound its way up the mountain face, and right through the stony isle.

Within moments most of the warriors of Knossos were dead, shrieking, aflame, nowhere to take cover. Merk watched in panic as a dragon singled him out and dove for him. Out of some primal reflex, he ducked, and the dragon's claw knocked the helmet off his head, sending it clanging down, bouncing off the rocks, down to the water. Yet somehow, miraculously, Merk survived, the flames parting ways around his massive shield as he crouched below it.

Merk saw dozens more dragons turning for them, and he knew that death was coming, that, within moments, whoever survived on this rocky isle would be dead. Their strategy had failed. They had been spared from the trolls only to be killed by the dragons.

Without thinking, Merk turned and ran. He saw Lorna standing there, frozen in panic, sheltered behind a stone ledge from the flames, most of her Watchers dead. At her side stood Thurn, still fighting off trolls valiantly, despite his multiple wounds.

Merk grabbed Lorna, yanked her, and forced her to run with him.

She turned and looked at Thurn.

He nodded back.

"Run!" he said. "It is your only chance."

"Only if you come!" she yelled.

She grabbed his wrist, and he turned and ran with them, covering their backs from any attack.

With the dragons closing in, the isle aflame, men dead all around them, they ran for their lives. Merk's heart slammed as he sensed the dragons closing in behind him and as he saw, in the distance, the far end of the isle. If they could just make it to the edge, to the far side of the fort, Merk knew, they could reach the cliffs on the far side of the isle, those that had real ocean beneath them, and not the sharp rocks and treacherous tides of the Bay of Death. From there they could leap safely.

A dragon dove down and set dozens of running warriors aflame beside them, the heat searing Merk's side, barely missing them. He gasped, sweating, realizing what a close call it was.

Merk turned and looked back over his shoulder, saw another dragon coming right for them, and knew that this time, the dragon would not miss. He and Lorna were about to die.

They reached the far side of the fort, and as they ducked behind its stone walls, the column of flame rolled past them, just missing by inches.

"There!" Merk cried.

They ran to the edge of the cliffs, and stopped short as they looked below. Merk's heart fell—it was a huge drop, perhaps a hundred feet, into the massive rolling waves of the ocean. There were no rocks, true, but the fall hardly seemed welcoming.

He stood there, hesitating. He hated heights. And he hated water. Thurn ran up behind them, turned and faced off against several trolls who were giving chase, swinging his chain and ball and killing them all before they could get close.

Merk turned and looked back and saw the dragons coming back again, he knew that staying here would mean a certain death. Already one singled them out, breathed its fire, and Merk, watched, in horror, as a wall of flame came right for them. Thurn, the bravest warrior he had ever seen, stood there proudly and made a stand, shielding them from the oncoming dragon.

"JUMP!" Thurn urged. "Go now, while you have a chance!"

Lorna squeezed his hand, and he saw the look of assurance in her eyes and it gave him strength. She prodded him, and they leapt together, holding hands.

The fire just missed them as they plummeted over the edge of the cliff. Merk found himself yelling as they fell and flailed through the air, all the way down until they hit the water. They had watched the waves, and had prayed that Lorna had timed it right so that they landed when a huge wave rolled in. Otherwise, the water would be too shallow and the fall would surely kill them.

They landed smack in the center of a big wave as it rolled in. The water was freezing, the tides unbelievably strong, and as Merk plunged below the surface, he wondered if every bone in his body was breaking.

He squeezed Lorna's hand beneath the surface, and as she fought the plunge and began kicking her way back up towards the surface, so did he. They kicked together, Merk's ears bursting, strange creatures brushing against him beneath the water, his lungs feeling as if they were crushed.

Then, finally, just when he thought he would drown, they surfaced.

Merk gasped for breath. He turned and looked in every direction, wiping water from his eyes. Corpses, of trolls, of men, floated in the water all around him, some still aflame. He looked up and saw the dragons descending for the isle of Knossos again, criss-crossing it, until it was one huge cauldron of flame. A few more seconds up there, and they would have been dead.

He saw Thurn, standing nobly up there, swinging his sword at the dragon even while he was aflame. Then, finally, he watched in horror as Thurn, aflame, fell backwards off the cliff, plummeting for the sea. He landed in a great hiss of steam, and Merk could not tell if he were dead or alive. He did not know how any human could have survived that.

Merk heard the awful sound of hundreds of good men dying up there, and he watched in horror as the dragons swept down, talons extended, and smashed the fort of Knossos into pieces. This sacred and proud place, which had stood for thousands of years, was no more.

As they bobbed in the waves, the undertow taking them out to sea, Merk looked out at the black, ominous waters and wondered if this ocean were even more dangerous than where they had left. He felt the undertow sucking everything down, saw the fins of the strange creatures out at sea, and he had a sinking feeling.

And then, just when he thought it could not get any worse, he looked up and saw several dragons had spotted them. They broke from the pack and dove down, right for them.

They roared, and a column of flame rolled down for them. Merk could already feel the heat. Paradoxically, they would be burned alive while in these freezing waters.

They squeezed hands and braced themselves, and Merk could not help but think: *What an awful way to die, where flame meets water.*

CHAPTER TWENTY EIGHT

Kyle sprinted beside Andor and Leo through the ravaged countryside of Escalon, heading north, determined to reach Kyra before she could fly to Marda. He could not shake the image from his mind of her flying overhead on the dragon, could not shake the feeling that she was flying to a place from which she would never return.

Kyle ran with all he had, running so fast that the countryside around him was a blur, running faster even than Andor, than Leo, faster than any human could. He was determined to stop her from entering Marda, a land where, he knew, her kind could not survive. Even with her skills, Kyra, he knew, was not prepared to face that kind of evil.

Yet he had to admit he had another, deeper reason for racing to find her. He could not deny what he had felt from the moment he had laid eyes on her. He was in love with her. He knew it in every ounce of his being. She was the girl he had been seeing in his mind's eye ever since he had been born, for hundreds of years, the girl he knew he was destined to be with. She was the one, he knew, that would change everything.

Kyle would not hesitate to give up his life to be with her. Ever since he had seen her, he could not explain it, but he knew his destiny was intertwined with hers. She was the one he had been waiting for, for thousands of years. The thought of losing her tore him to pieces. He would do whatever he had to do, even if it meant heading into the darkest depths of Marda, even if he had to walk through the Flames himself, to bring her back.

Kyle reflected on how lucky he had been to rescue her from that massive battle against the Pandesians, the trolls, how lucky he had been to survive that himself, due only to the dragons' intervention. He felt something monumental shifting in the universe, that they were on the brink of history, of the world being either saved or destroyed for good. And he could not help but feel as if he and Kyra were in the crossroads. After all these centuries, the Final Coming was here. It was the time he had learned of as a child, the time he had thought would never arrive. These were the days the sky would turn black with dragons, the oceans would spit fire, and the rivers would run with blood. He remembered the prophecies and remembered wondering if they were but myths. Yet now, as he looked around and saw the destruction in Escalon, he knew these were no myths.

Kyle continued to sprint, passing entire charred villages, piles of corpses, a land once so beautiful now torn to shreds. He leapt over gaping fissures in the earth, pits left where the dragons had sliced open the land with their talons; he ran through forests twisted and black, burned to ashes. He passed through a land he barely recognized, crossing it at nearly the speed of light. Marda, he knew, lay just ahead, and he redoubled his efforts.

Yet as he neared the Flames, something tugged at him, and he felt himself tremble with a premonition. It was like a pulse, or a vibration, and it was pulling him in another direction. As he ran it became stronger, so strong he could not ignore it, like a bell tolling that he could not ignore.

Baffled, Kyle turned and looked west, wondering what it could be. In that direction, somewhere over the horizon, lay the Tower of Ur. As he looked, he felt it again, racing through his veins. It was a call of distress. An urgent call for help.

Kyle stopped, at a crossroads, no longer sure what to do. He looked north, knowing the Flames lay just over the horizon, and somewhere beyond them, Kyra. Yet everything inside of him was also screaming at him to turn west. One of his brothers was in grave danger, a danger he could not ignore.

It made no sense to Kyle. The tower had been destroyed. Who could possibly be west, in the Tower of Ur? What danger could they be in?

As agonizing as it was, it did not give Kyle a choice. He turned away from running toward Marda, and instead allowed turned west. Someone beyond those hills needed him—someone who was connected to Kyra—and he could not abandon them.

*

Kyle finished sprinting up a series of rolling hills and as he crested the last one, he stopped short at what he saw before him, stunned at the sight: there, against the setting sun, a nation of trolls was flooding the countryside. Kyle's heart stopped in his throat.

That could only mean one thing: The Flames were lowered. Vesuvius must have crossed the Devil's Finger. He must have beaten Merk and reached the Tower of Kos before him. And he must have stolen the Sword of Fire.

Even worse, there, down in the valley, Kyle spotted a small group of people standing before the destroyed tower. He blinked, confused, wondering who it could be, and then he recognized one of them: Kolva. Kyra's uncle. A fellow Watcher, one of the legendary Watchers of all time, facing off against the trolls—and entirely surrounded. Standing beside him were two people whom Kyle did not recognize, and the three of them were about to die. Now Kyle understood why he had been summoned here.

Without thinking, Kyle sprinted down the hill, Andor and Leo at his side. He burst into the trolls, running faster than he'd ever had, raised his staff, and as he reached the army, he turned the staff sideways and smashed into the lines of trolls.

Sparks flew from his staff as dozens of trolls went flying back. He swung again and again, the blows so powerful they sent dozens more trolls flying through the air, hundreds of feet. Beside him, Leo and Andor leapt into the air, snarling, sinking fangs into the trolls all around them, tearing them to pieces and watching Kyle's back.

Kyle smashed his way through the stunned nation of trolls until finally he cleared room and fought his way all the way to Kolva and his two companions. He leapt forward and jabbed a troll right before it could stab Kolva, while Leo and Andor jumped on two trolls from behind before they could smash the two others with their halberds, saving them just in time.

Kyle had no chance, though, to catch his breath. He turned to see another wave of trolls pouring in. He swung his staff again and again, smashing one troll, then another, then another. He leapt into the air over three of them, kicked a dozen more to the ground, then spun and struck a dozen more. He fought like a man on fire, determined to save his friends' lives, to fend off these beasts, to protect his homeland, and all around him, trolls fell. The perimeter widened with each blow.

Soon he had felled hundreds of them.

Beside him, Kolva caught a second wind and fought boldly, too, as did his two companions. Kolva wielded his staff, expertly taking out dozens of trolls, while the man and woman with him grabbed flails off the ground and swung them wildly, killing dozens more. They all seemed liberated to have been rescued, to have a second chance at life, and Kyle felt elated that he had trusted his instincts and come here.

Kyle felt himself gaining momentum. They created a wider perimeter around the Tower of Ur, and he was feeling optimistic that maybe he would be able to drive this army back to Marda, to make a stand on behalf of all of Escalon. This, after all, was the real front line for his homeland, where the real war was being fought.

Yet as he fought, an ominous horn sounded, rising over the shouts of dying trolls, and as Kyle looked out, he was aghast at what he saw: hundreds of trees fell with a great whooshing noise as the forest opened up all around him. Tens of thousands more trolls poured forward.

Kyle felt a chill of dread; there was no way they could defend against this many trolls.

Kyle swung his staff again and again, dropping trolls by the dozens, but even as he did, he knew it was futile. This was no mere army—this was an entire nation. He had thrown himself to Kolva's defense—only to walk into a death for himself.

As he fought, Kyle found himself growing weaker. His blows had less power, and the trolls were getting closer. He was increasingly surrounded from all sides, and to his shock, he felt an awful pain in his shoulder and realized a troll had gotten close enough to slice his arm with his halberd. Kyle killed the troll at once, jabbing it in the forehead with his staff, yet it did not change the fact that Kyle had become vulnerable. His aura of invincibility was quickly disappearing.

As thousands more trolls broke through the forest, stampeding each other, Kyle saw his death looming before him. He heard a cry and he looked over in horror to see Kolva drop to his knees, a troll's halberd in his stomach. He watched, helpless, as Kolva began to die.

The man and woman beside him fell, too, each knocked down by the handle of a troll's halberd, each prone on the ground, helpless to do anything but await their deaths. Even Leo and Andor were surrounded now, the crowd too thick for them to fight back, their whines audible as they were injured.

Kyle, gasping for air, knew that he was staring death in the face. After all these centuries, his time had come. And his final thought was not that he regretted dying—only that he regretted not seeing Kyra's face again.

CHAPTER TWENTY NINE

Kyra hiked cautiously through the black wood, crouching beneath the huge thorns, on edge, the gloom pervasive and the sense of evil oppressive. It was so dark here it felt like night, the twilight barely able to penetrate the canopy of gnarled branches. Beneath her feet, the ash soil and gnarled, dead branches made odd crunching noises, adding to the feeling of death.

Kyra peered into the thick wood, trying to make sense of this place, unlike any she had ever been. The trees were entangled with vines, twisting and stretching in every direction, interlacing the branches, protruding with thorns nearly as large as she. As she walked, the canopy dropped so low that in some places she nearly had to duck. The forest seemed too narrow, the branches and thorns creeping ever closer to the path, scratching her arms.

Kyra heard a perpetual rattling inside the thicket, the stirring of creatures, and it kept her on edge. She spotted glowing yellow and red eyes hiding in the blackness, staring back at her, and she gripped her staff, expecting an attack at any moment, feeling as if she were walking into the blackest corners of hell.

Kyra hiked and hiked, her heart pounding, wondering where the path was leading her, when finally she saw, somewhere up ahead, the faintest glow. Obscured behind the branches, it was like the glow of a torch, or a fire, so faint, appearing and disappearing. She felt drawn to it, the first marker she had seen in the gloom. It encouraged her to keep hiking, to keep following the trail. As she went, her feet sank into the slimy, soft earth beneath her, made of something like moss, sinking up to her ankles.

She suddenly heard a noise and raised her staff and spun to see a black, wraithlike creature floating in the air. It looked like a ghost, or a demon, all black, with gray eyes. As it hovered behind her, she jabbed it with her staff, and it made an awful howling noise before disappearing into the air above her head, winding its way through the thickets.

Heart pounding, unsettled, Kyra turned back and continued on her way, winding deeper and deeper into the wood. She felt a new feeling beneath her feet, a crunching, and she looked down to see a trail of bones. She heard a creaking noise, and she looked up at the trees and was horrified to see, swinging there, the rotting carcasses of people who had traveled here. Others were impaled on branches, displayed like trophies. It was like walking through a mausoleum.

Soon, the trail smoothed out, and Kyra had a sinking feeling. The trail was fresh here, untouched. It was virgin territory. Clearly, no one else had ever gotten this far in the wood before. There must, she knew, be a reason.

Kyra proceeded deeper, heart pounding, until finally she turned a corner and the canopy rose, opened into a clearing. She was able to stand taller, the gnarled branches now rising up a good thirty feet, as the forest opened wider here. Up ahead, perhaps a hundred yards in the distance, she saw the definitive glow of the torch, and she felt a sense of relief.

As she neared the end of the trail, a wall of thorns, against flickering torchlight she just barely made out a figure, perhaps a man, perhaps something else. It stood there, its back to her, wearing a black hooded cloak, hunched over a flame. Her sense of apprehension deepened. She could sense the evil even from where she stood.

Kyra stood there, heart pounding, tightening her grip on her staff. She wondered why the forest had ended, where she had arrived, and if she would ever get out. The person before her was definitely some sort of creature; he possessed an intense spiritual energy, making the hair on her skin rise in warning. She sensed he was a spiritual master, and one from the dark side. Worst of all, she could sense he was more powerful than she.

A deep voice cut through the air.

"Kyra, the great one, has finally come to my den."

The voice was dark and gravelly, sounding more like the voice of a creature than a man, setting her hairs on end. His back was still to her, only deepening her sense of apprehension.

Slowly, the creature turned, and Kyra felt dread as she saw that he had the body of a man, but the head of a goat, with sharpened hooves for hands. He looked at Kyra and smiled an evil smile. He was the most grotesque thing she had ever seen, and as he spoke, her stomach tightened in a knot.

"Your mother is not here to protect you now, is she?" he asked.

As he spoke, a long, snake-like tongue slipped out the side of his mouth.

"No. You're in Marda now, in the Thicket of Thorns. You're beyond anyone's protection. You have come to a place you should never have come, and you have come uninvited. Did you really think the Staff of Truth would sit unguarded? Did you truly think you could just walk in here and steal it from us?"

He laughed, a grating, ominous sound. Kyra tried to steady her breath, to calm herself, to focus on the adversary before her.

"I have stood guard for thousands of years," he continued, "and have protected it from people far more powerful than you. *You*," he said with derision, "a lame girl, with a few powers you don't even understand."

Kyra flinched, yet forced herself to stay strong, to stand her ground and to speak back firmly.

"I sense the weapon lies beyond that wall," she said, impressed by the strength in her voice, which did not match her inward fears. "I will give you one warning: you can move aside now, or I will kill you."

He laughed, an awful sound that sank into her soul.

"Brave words for a terrified girl," he replied. "I can sense your fear even from here. I can nearly taste it. You *should* be afraid. You should be *very* afraid. Have a look at my feet."

She looked down and saw, at his feet, a pile of bones, some ancient and some new, and her apprehension deepened.

"They thought they were stronger than me, too," he said. "Your bones shall make a most delicious snack. Of that, I am sure."

Listening to him, Kyra sensed that this was more than just an encounter. This was a test. A test that she would have to pass by life or by death.

Suddenly the creature nodded and raised his hooves, and as he did, Kyra heard an awful screech. From out of the thickets there suddenly flew down four awful creatures, resembling owls, but with claws twice as long, sharp fangs, and as large as she. She felt a wave of panic, and she knew she had to stay strong, to rise above her fear, above any emotion, if she were to win. This was not a test of her skills, she realized; it was about her inner strength. Her powers. Her control over her mind.

Kyra focused on the creatures before her. The first came at her, swooping down and lowering its claws for her face, and she swung her staff and cracked it in the nose. It dropped with a screech to the ground.

Kyra ducked as another dove for her head, then reached around and cracked that one in its ribs, sending it skidding across the soil.

The third attacked Kyra from behind, circling around and scratching her in the back. She screeched in pain, caught off guard; yet she quickly gathered herself, dropping to her knees, rolling on the ground, then wheeling around and smashing the beast across the face. It screeched and fell at her feet.

One final creature was still circling, and as it lunged for her, screeching, she jumped to her feet, grabbed her staff, stepped sideways, and jabbed the beast in the throat. It fell down, dead at her feet.

Kyra was surprised to hear a screech behind her, and she realized, too late, that a fifth beast had been unleashed. It came at her before she could react, grabbed her shirt with its claws, and hoisted her into the air. She swung at it as it carried her, yet was helpless to reach it.

The beast flew with her, driving her forward, aiming to smash her into the thicket of thorns. She saw a huge, sharp thorn about to pierce her chest, and at the last second she twisted, just missing it, smashing into the wall of vines instead.

She was lucky, she knew, to miss it, as she dropped onto the floor, aching in every part of her body. The beast gave her no time to recover; it lunged down and opened its mouth, ready to finish her off.

Kyra rolled out of the way at the last second, spun around, and grabbed its slimy, disgusting scales with two hands. She kept it at bay, wrestling with it, then finally managed to hurl it into a thorn beside her. It shrieked as she impaled it through its mouth. It finally hung there, dead.

Kyra, breathing hard, aching, turned, grabbed her staff, and prepared to face off against the creature that summoned them.

He stared back, frowning, clearly surprised.

"Impressive," he said. "But you're still just a girl. And I am the all-powerful Koo."

Koo pulled his hood lower, stepped forward, and suddenly there was a ball of fire in his hand. He threw it at her, and as the fire rushed for her face, she ducked. It barely missed, setting the woods behind her aflame.

He threw another ball, and another, and another. She kept dodging, summoning her powers, using her instincts to be faster than the flames. She was in a place of deep focus, a place where she was not in complete control of her own body, her own actions.

She managed to dodge all his fireballs, yet soon she felt the tremendous heat behind her. All around her, the woods were aflame.

Infuriated he could not hit her, the beast suddenly hoisted a black staff covered with thorns, an ominous weapon. He stepped forward and faced her.

Snarling, he swung for her head, and she raised her staff and blocked it. As she did, the thick spikes of his staff impaled her staff, and he managed to yank it out of her hands.

Kyra stood there, defenseless, appalled, stripped of her staff. He laughed back at her as he threw her staff down to the floor. He then charged, raising the spiked staff high and swinging for her throat.

Kyra dodged, feeling the thorns graze her skin, realizing how close it had come, how fast he was. With the woods aflame behind her, her time was running out and she had nowhere left to run.

He lunged at her, jabbing at her stomach, and she looked down and saw a blade at the end of it. Before she could dodge, it stabbed her in the stomach.

Kyra gasped, stunned, the pain blinding. For a moment she couldn't breathe, and her whole world went blind.

She sank to her knees onto the soft forest floor, and he dug the blade deeper and deeper in her stomach. She felt the tears gush out—tears of pain, tears of failure, tears of surprise. She had never expected to die here.

Kyra looked up and saw him grinning, satisfied, jamming the blade in more, turning it in her stomach, and she knew she was dying, and in an awful way. What an awful place to die, she thought, here in this place, where no one will ever find me. She would be just one more set of bones on a pile of bones.

"You see, Kyra," Koo growled. "No one has ever defeated me. And no one ever will. You are not strong enough. *You are not strong enough,*" he insisted.

Something in his words summoned something in her. She hated being told what she wasn't capable of. It spurred a defiance deep within her, a deep desire to prove others wrong. All her life, as the only girl in a fort filled with men, she had been told she wasn't good enough.

Not strong enough.

She turned the words around in her mind. There was no such thing as defeat, she knew, unless you accepted it. Unless you *chose* to believe, to accept, you were not strong enough. And she refused to accept it. She could rise above defeat, she knew. She could be as strong as she wanted to be. As strong as she *believed* herself to be.

Kyra a felt heat rising within her. It was a heat of rejection. A rejection of death. A rejection of weakness. She did not deserve to die. For the first time, in her life, she truly felt that. Who was anybody else to say she deserved to die? She was entitled to life.

Suddenly, Kyra felt herself changing, felt the momentum shifting the other way. Instead of getting weaker, she felt herself getting stronger. Instead of the pain, she felt herself rising above the pain. She felt herself, amazingly, becoming stronger.

Pain is only pain, she heard her mind say, a mantra within herself. *And when we lose our fear of pain, there is nothing anyone can do to harm us. When we don't fear pain, we no longer fear anything. If we embrace the pain, stop resisting it, rise above it, we are all-powerful. Limitless.*

Kyra found herself reaching out and grabbing his staff of thorns. The thorns dimly hurt her hand as her fingers bled, yet she refused to pay attention. Instead, she squeezed the staff, and slowly retracted it from her body.

The monster stared back in disbelief as she extracted the blade, one inch at a time, her arms shaking. Finally she extracted the entire staff and threw it to the ground.

She stood upright, forcing herself to stand proud and strong, and faced the monster. She felt bigger than the pain. And she knew she had reached a new level of her power, the level that she had been most afraid to face, and that nothing on this planet could harm her now.

Kyra reached down, laid her two palms on the wound on her stomach, closed her eyes, and breathed. She took a deep breath in, saw white light rushing through her veins, into her wound, and she felt the healing power being summoned from deep within her.

She did not even need to look down as she opened her eyes. She knew her stomach was now completely healed. Indeed, she felt stronger than before.

The monster stared back in utter shock, his mouth agape.

Kyra did not give Koo a chance to regroup. She stepped forward and kicked him with both feet in the chest.

The monster stumbled back into the branches and shrieked as he caught fire, the flames roaring all around him.

"I refuse your death sentence," Kyra said, feeling stronger than she'd ever had, feeling as if she'd overcome something within herself. "I deserve life."

The creature, in a rage, rose to his feet, shrieked, and lunged for her.

But this time, Kyra felt bigger than herself. As the beast charged, Kyra felt the heat within consume her, and this time she let it overtake her. She found herself filled with a power she could scarcely understand, found herself doing things she never would have been able to before, as she sidestepped, dodging his lightning-fast strike, and jabbed him in the face with her staff, knocking him flat on his back.

He jumped back to his feet and charged, leaping into the air for her. She was faster, though, able to anticipate it, and she rushed forward and struck him in the stomach, reaching him first, knocking him flat on his back.

It spun around and grabbed its staff and jumped to its feet, swinging wildly at her. But Kyra backed up, dodging him easily, feeling faster, stronger. He raised the staff higher with both hands, preparing to bring it down for her neck, and she lunged forward and struck him in the throat.

He dropped his staff of thorns and this time, she caught it in midair. Koo stood there, disarmed, shocked, defenseless. And she rushed forward and jabbed the staff through his heart.

Koo gasped, mouth open, blood pouring from it, as he looked back at her in utter shock.

Then he dropped down to its knees, dead.

As he did, the final wall of thorns opened up, the fire still blazing all around her.

146

Kyra stepped through the opening, right before the fire completely consumed the wood.

She had won. Victory was hers.

Kyra found herself standing on a ledge, a small plateau high up on a cliff. The horizon opened up, the sky a twilight streaked with scarlet red, and for the first time, the entire landscape of Marda unfolded before her. She saw a massive city spread out before her, a megalopolis. It was a city of death, outlined in shades of black.

And somewhere down there, she knew, she just knew, lay the Staff of Truth, waiting for her.

CHAPTER THIRTY

Duncan emerged from the canyon, flanked by Kavos, Bramthos, Seavig, Anvin and Arthfael and several hundred of his men, all, he was honored to see, eager to join him on the most dangerous mission of his life. As they reached the desert floor, Duncan looked and saw, just north, beyond the open field, the massive sprawl of the Pandesian army. There they camped, a sea of black on the horizon, banners flapping in the wind, a silhouette in the breaking dawn. The time had come to risk it all, to instigate them in the open field, and to lure them back down into the canyon.

The mission, Duncan knew, was foolhardy. His chances of luring them down into the canyon were slim; if they attacked before they could lure them down, they would surely not survive. And his chances of emerging from the other side of the canyon after doing so were even more slim. Yet it had to be done. Luring the Pandesians down to the bottom of the canyon was the only way, and if he died at the bottom, drowned with them, then so be it.

Duncan led his men as they marched through the wasteland, until finally, he motioned. They all came to a sudden stop, lined up in perfect discipline, their armor softly rattling in the pre-dawn silence. No sound was audible other than that of a vulture screaming high overhead, no doubt anticipating the meal to come. Duncan raised his hand for quiet as the rattling of their armor finally grew still, all of them standing there, watching Duncan, as he watched the horizon. He was determined not to make a mistake.

Duncan watched the horizon, saw, in the distance, the faint outline of black. There were all the banners of the Pandesian army, flapping in the wind as far as they could see. He scanned the skies, saw the dragons had long gone, and he knew the Pandesians had regrouped, were preparing to attack again. Of course they would: Ra never forgot an enemy.

Within moments, as Duncan suspected, a horn sounded. There came another, and another, all the Pandesian horns echoing each other up and down the ranks. They were horns designed to intimidate, horns that had been used to vanquish all throughout the Empire, in every land and country, as the Pandesians obliterated whoever stood before them. They were horns meant to embolden the Pandesian army, to urge the great beast to move forward.

And that was exactly what Duncan wanted.

The Pandesian army began to march, a great rumble, stretching across the horizon, all heading right for Duncan and his men. Duncan stood there, his heart slamming, watching death approach. He willed them closer.

"Hold the line!" Duncan commanded, feeling the uneasiness amongst his men.

Yet they listened. He saw some of his younger soldiers antsy, shifting in place. They would need discipline for this, discipline to hold the line, to face down a much greater army out in the open field, to let them approach. They would need more discipline than they'd ever had in their lives.

Duncan stood there and waited, the army getting closer with each step, the desert black with soldiers. The sound of their elephants rumbled above all, followed by the sound of horses. The sound of soldiers marching trailed that, and then, finally, as they neared, but a few hundred yards away, there came the sound of their banners, flapping violently in the desert wind.

As they neared, Duncan could see the hunger in their eyes, the bloodlust. He could also see the greed: for them, their prey stood helpless before them. They must have assumed that Duncan had come to surrender.

Duncan watched more of his men shift uncomfortably, as the Pandesians came nearly a hundred yards away.

"HOLD THE LINE!" he boomed.

His men stopped shifting and stood there, boldly, bravely, facing the oncoming death. Duncan was proud of them. They had to let the much bigger army get closer. They had to appeal to their sense of greed. In his experience, armies always overreached when they saw an easy kill. It blinded their judgment.

Finally, when the Pandesians were fifty yards away, Duncan's heart slamming in his chest, he shouted:

"RETREAT!"

His men all turned and sprinted back toward the canyon. Duncan wanted the Pandesians to think that he had changed his mind and fled in terror.

It worked. Behind him, as he hoped, there came a great stampede, a great rumbling of elephants and horses. They were closing in, pursuing them, nearly faster than his men could run.

Duncan gasped for air as he and the others reached the canyon edge and immediately began to descend. They slipped and slid down the steep wall, navigating the tricky terrain until they wound their way all the way down to the canyon floor. Duncan craned his neck and looked up to see the Pandesian army right on their heels, pursuing them, reaching the edge of the canyon, pausing, and looking down, blood in their eyes, before resuming their chase and following them down the canyon on foot.

"TO THE OTHER SIDE!" Duncan boomed.

His men sprinted with him across the canyon floor, and Duncan looked over shoulder to see the Pandesians filing down, filling the canyon, pursuing them, just as he had hoped.

Having done what he had set out to, Duncan knew the first part was a success. But now came the hardest part: he'd have to sprint with his men across the canyon and ascend the other side.

Duncan reached the far wall, the rock slippery in his sweaty palms, and looked back, heart pounding, to see the Pandesians closing in, letting out a shout of victory and bloodlust.

"CLIMB!" he cried.

Duncan began the climb with his men, heart pounding, realizing how risky this was. He looked up and saw the steep ascent before them, and knew that just one slip would mean falling back down into death's arms. He wondered if they could make it.

Worse, if Aidan and the men of Leptus were unsuccessful, if they did not reach Everfall and could not flood the canyon, then the army behind him would surely kill him, and all his men. And if they did flood the canyon but if Duncan did not ascend and get out of the way of the raging waters soon enough, then he and his men could be drowned, too.

Duncan suddenly heard the sound of metal chipping stone, and he turned, alert, to see the Pandesians, so close now, spears raised. They hurled them, and one just missed Duncan's exposed back, chipping the stone beside him, and as he looked up and saw how far they had left to go, he suddenly realized that they would die an even worse death than he thought.

CHAPTER THIRTY ONE

Alec stood at the bow of the ship, gripping the rail with one hand and the Unfinished Sword with the other, ocean spray hitting him in the face as their huge ship rose and fell in the turbulent waters of the Bay of Death. He had a knot in his stomach as he reentered his homeland, filled with dread to be entering Escalon again since the invasion. He knew what was awaiting him, and he felt as if he were sailing to his death.

The Bay of Death hardly set him at ease, either. He had never sailed a body of water even remotely like this one, its waters so black, dotted with the white foam caps of whirlpools, spraying everywhere as the wind ripped off the water. The currents were wild and unpredictable, throwing their ship from side to side, then suddenly up and down. They crashed into wave after wave, and he was hardly able to get his footing.

Alec looked behind him and took solace in seeing the fleet from the Lost Isles following, all of them having sailed for days to cross the Sea of Tears. Beside him stood their leader, while on his other side stood Sovos, all staring intently at the waters ahead and gripping the rails, knowing life and death hung in the balance.

Alec looked out ahead, and the sight made his blood run cold. The sky was filled with dragons, screeching, diving down low then up high again, spitting fire down into the sea and circling the isle of Knossos, the legendary fort. They rained down fire on it and smashed it with their talons as if they wanted to tear it to shreds.

Alec watched as a dragon dove down and with its long talons sliced away a whole section of the fort. A great rumble followed as boulders rolled down the cliffs and crashed into the bay.

Down below, in the waters, the sight was no more reassuring: thousands of trolls floated in the waters, dead, burned or sliced to death, while hundreds more human warriors shrieked and fell off the cliffs, trying unsuccessfully to escape the dragons' wrath.

It was a scene of chaos and death. Alec studied it confusion, wondering what had happened here. It appeared that an army of trolls had invaded, had attacked the small isle of Knossos, and Alec wondered why. He wondered how the trolls could have made it this far south.

Most of all, he was stunned by the dragons. He had never seen a real dragon in his life, and he had not even been truly sure they existed until now. He wondered how they could have reached Escalon, where they had come from. He wondered how his beloved country could have changed so quickly. He had left but weeks before, and now it was a land torn apart, a land he barely recognized, filled with monsters and death.

Alec felt a deepening sense of apprehension as he witnessed the power of those beasts. He clutched the sword in his hand, felt it vibrating, and he looked down at it, surprised as always. It had begun to glow, and it seemed to be pointing up at the sky. At the dragons.

Alec felt a rush of energy flow through his hand, his wrist, his arm, and he wondered. Could a weapon really harm a dragon? Was he truly meant to wield it? It felt, as he held it, as if the sword were leading them right into the very heart of chaos and destruction.

Suddenly, Alec had a realization. He turned to Sovos.

"This is no mistake," he said. "You are sailing us right toward the dragons."

Sovos nodded silently, still looking straight ahead, and Alec was mortified.

"But why? Do you wish to kill us all?"

Sovos ignored him.

"It is because of the Sword, isn't it?" Alec asked, piecing it all together. Alec grabbed his arm, demanding. "You think this Sword can save us?"

Sovos still ignored him, and Alec felt a rush of fear and outrage.

"Do you really expect to attack a flock of dragons with a single sword?" Alec asked. "And do you expect me to lead that attack?"

Finally, Sovos turned to him.

"You are the only hope we have," he answered gravely.

Alec heard an awful screech, looked up at the skies, and he felt a sense of awe at the thought. Looking up at those massive creatures circling high above, those ancient, primordial beasts who had lived for thousands of years, he could not conceive how a simple sword could make any difference, could even scratch the smallest of their scales.

Alec gripped the Sword tighter.

"And if you're wrong?" Alec asked, gulping.

Sovos shook his head.

"If we are wrong," he said, looking grimly out to sea, "then all of us will die. They will find us, whether it is on Escalon or the Lost Isles. Fleeing is not an option."

He turned to Alec and laid a hand on his shoulder.

"You must try, Alec," he said. "Legend has always told that the sword, if forged, could fend off a dragon. The time has come to put legend to the test."

Alec gripped the rail as a massive wave rolled beneath the ship, raising it up, and he felt sick as they all came splashing down. Inch by painful inch they sailed closer to the isle, to the flock of dragons. He heard a sudden thumping down below, and he searched the waters to see scores of bodies, humans and trolls, floating face-up, the currents carrying them away. It was a macabre scene, one Alec already wanted to wipe from his mind.

The currents shifted strongly, and they skirted Knossos, to the left of the isle, circling behind it. As they did, Alec narrowed his eyes and spotted two bodies in the water, flailing amidst the torrential currents. Unlike all the other bodies, these were alive.

"Survivors!" Alec called out. "Do you see?"

The others pressed close and stared into the waters, and finally, they spotted them, too. Alec saw a man with a short beard and the hardened face of a mercenary floating beside the most beautiful woman he had ever seen. This unlikely couple were holding onto each other, keeping each other afloat. And they stared up at the sky in terror.

Alec looked up, wondering, and before he could even see it, he heard the ear-splitting roar. He looked up, horrified, to see a massive dragon, diving down right for them. It reached out with its talons and opened its great mouth, revealing rows of sharpened teeth, some of them longer than Alec.

Alec stood there, trembling, forcing himself to overcome his fear. He felt the Sword pulsing in his palm, and it gave him strength. He knew this was the time. The time for courage. The time for life and death. The time to save these people.

As they sailed ever closer to the dragon, he sensed that he, the smith of this sword, was the only one who could wield this weapon, who could change the fate of Escalon.

"We all die," Sovos said, turning to him, his eyes a piercing blue, aglow with adrenaline and terror. "The question is, how? This is your moment to decide. Will you die boldly? Or will you shrink to your death, as a coward?"

Alec stood there, feeling the power of the Sword ripple through him, up and down his arms, through his entire body, and he realized how insane this was. He, a lone boy from a small village, a nobody, facing off with a dragon with a simple sword.

And yet the dragon dove down, and he felt in his heart he could not let these people die. He made his decision.

Rushing forward, Alec jumped up on the beam, ran to the very edge of the rail, placed each foot firmly on a narrow strip of wood so that he had his footing, and faced the enemy. Waves splashed at his feet as he stood there, high above the others, legs apart, firmly planted and holding out the Sword.

The dragon suddenly looked up at him, forgetting its victims down below, and shrieked, as if infuriated at the sight of the Sword. It changed course, diving straight down for Alec instead.

A moment later, it released a stream of flame.

Alec turned his head and braced himself, expecting to be burnt alive, and raised the sword out before him.

Yet suddenly, to his shock, the flames stopped in midair. They stopped as if hitting a wall, twenty yards away from him—and then they disappeared.

The dragon looked just as shocked as Alec was.

Yet still, it continued to fly, scowling, opening its jaws wider, focusing only on him. It opened its wings wide and flew ever closer, as if to swallow him. Soon the dragon was but feet away, Alec's entire world dark beneath its shadow.

Alec knew this was his only chance. His heart slamming, suppressing his fear, he shrieked a great battle cry and leapt from the ship, holding the Sword out before him. He jumped up, right into the dragon's mouth, and drove the sword straight up, into the roof of the dragon's palate, driving it in with all his might.

Blood poured down in rivers as the dragon shrieked an awful noise, the vibration of it ejecting Alec from its mouth and sending him tumbling head over heels into the sea.

And as he swirled in the relentless waters of the Bay of Death, the last thing he saw was the great dragon, so alive but moments before, closing its eyes and plummeting into the sea, beside him, despite every possible logic, dead.

CHAPTER THIRTY TWO

Vesuvius flailed in the raging waters of the Bay of Death, gasping for air as the wild currents nearly sucked him down. He swam his way back up to the surface after each current dragged him under and, exhausted, wounded, he knew he couldn't last long. All around him there floated the dead bodies of his army of trolls, and it was like one big floating grave.

Vesuvius heard a rushing noise, and he glanced over his shoulder and was struck with terror to see a looming whirlpool, its whitecaps visible over the blackened water. In the other direction dragons screeched, diving and rising, crossing the sky with flame and breathing fire down into the waters, sending up columns of steam. Death awaited him on all sides.

Vesuvius could not believe he had found himself in this position. But moments ago his men were overtaking Knossos, closing in on Lorna, the warriors, about to wipe them all out and claim total victory. He had been so close to completing his victory, to destroying any last remnants of the rebels, to discovering what else that girl had been guarding in the tower, to learning how to keep the Flames down forever. It had all been right at his fingertips.

Then the dragons had appeared, and everything had changed. It had been a massacre, and he had been lucky to escape with his life, diving off the cliff and using his trolls to cushion his fall. Yet now here he was, suffering the first defeat of his life, floating at sea, barely clinging to life, all his dreams crushed.

Yet he refused to die. Not here, and not in this place. Vesuvius knew he had more death and destruction to wreak upon the world, and his job was unfinished. He certainly would not die until he had first vanquished the people of Escalon. He had to make them pay, all of them, and he would not let it end like this. He had been in worse positions before—and he had always survived. Death was terrible—but he was, he knew, more terrible than death.

As Vesuvius began to get sucked into the whirlpool's currents, he heard a shout, looked over, and saw nearby a few other trolls who had survived. His generals. They had loyally stayed by his side at every step, determined to protect him, helping to prop him up as best they could. Seeing them gave Vesuvius had an idea.

He suddenly twisted around, grabbed a general, and shoved him, sending him face-first into the whirlpool instead. The general shrieked as the waters began to suck him down, a look of shock and betrayal on his face. At the same, while he began to sink, Vesuvius leaned back and kicked off of him, using his leverage to send the general flying into the hole—and to kick himself away from the swirling current.

The move gave Vesuvius just enough momentum to swim away from the currents. He swam furiously, and within moments he was out of harm's way. He heard the general's muffled shrieks and watched him get sucked under for good. At least the troll had died in good service.

Vesuvius, bobbing wildly in the waters, set his sights on the rocky shore up ahead, on the far side of the bay, where so many of his trolls had washed up dead. He kicked and flailed and managed to grab hold of a large piece of flotsam. Finally, he could float.

For the first time, he breathed easy, resting his aching shoulders for a moment as he held onto the plank, bobbing up and down in the waters. It gave him the second wind he needed. He kicked, and this time, he caught the current and found himself on a rolling wave that crested high, then brought him crashing down low, all the while carrying him closer to shore.

He braced himself as the jagged rocks loomed and he came rushing right for the edge of the shore. Yet there was nothing he could do stop it.

Vesuvius smashed into the rocks, the pain so intense he thought all his bones were cracking. Yet in a sense, he enjoyed the pain. It made him feel alive again. He enjoyed feeling pain as much as he enjoyed inflicting it upon others.

Vesuvius shrieked, overcoming the pain, reached out and grabbed hold of a crack in the rocks, his hands slipping, holding on for dear life. As the currents threatened to carry him back out to sea, he held on for dear life, slipping on the moss. Finally, losing his grip, he reached out and snatched the floating plank beside him, then held it out and jammed it in the rocks.

He held on for dear life as a huge wave rushed back out to sea, trying to carry him. But he held on, and Vesuvius, this time, was safe.

Vesuvius quickly clambered up the rocks, breathing hard, arms shaking, until he finally collapsed onto the shore. He dropped down face-first on the rocky shore, amidst all the corpses, the only troll left alive in a sea of dead bodies.

And before he collapsed, there was one thing he knew for certain: he would live. At all costs, he would live. And he would wreak havoc on Escalon unlike any they had ever seen.

CHAPTER THIRTY THREE

Aidan held on tight as his horse galloped across the wasteland, riding beside Anvin, Leifall and the hundreds of men of Leptus, as they had for hours. Covered in dust, gasping for air, White keeping pace at their feet, finally they crested a hill and Aidan saw what they had come for: the towering cliffs of Everfall.

Aidan was awed by the sight. The cliffs rose from the wasteland like a monument to the heavens, and gushing and roaring down them were the largest waterfalls he had ever seen. It was spectacular. Their roar was deafening. Even from here, he felt himself sprayed with mist, the cool air and water so refreshing, cooling him down from the trek.

Aidan dismounted with the others and stood there, looking up, taking it all in. Water gushed down from hundreds of feet high, from impossibly high cliffs, smashing into rocks, creating huge columns of spray and coursing into a raging river which wound its way out past Leptus and toward the Bay of Death. Aidan could hardly believe that things like this even existed in nature, so beautiful, so awe-inspiring, and seemingly untouched by any human hand.

He thought of his father's plan to divert the water, to force it to change direction, to gush down the other side, and seeing it now, in person, it seemed impossible. Looking at it, so ancient, so powerful, Aidan doubted these waters could ever be made to change course. If they did, it seemed, they would flood the world.

"And now?" Anvin asked Leifall, shouting over the falls to be heard.

"We must go for the levers," Leifall replied. "Follow me."

Leifall hurried off at a brisk walk, his men following, and Aidan, too, followed, as he strutted around to the far side of the cliffs. Aidan found himself walking carefully on rock, slick with spray, slipping several times, the gushing noise ever louder, getting wetter by the second.

Finally, they reached the far side of the cliffs, and Leifall led them to a hidden cave. They ducked at the entrance, and Aidan followed them in.

Aidan found himself standing with the others inside an expansive cave, the arched ceiling rising thirty feet, the sound of the falls muted in here. He blinked as he adjusted to the dark, and as he did, he watched Leifall walk over to an enormous stone lever.

Anvin came over and studied it in wonder. Leifall turned to him.

"Built by our ancestors, for times of war," Leifall said.

"What does it do?" Anvin asked.

"Pull it, and the great stones of Everfall will open. The falls can be redirected. A new river will form, and the land will change forever."

Aidan stared in wonder.

"Can they reach my father?" he asked, hopeful. "Can they flood the canyon?"

Leifall looked back, grave.

"I do not know," he replied. "This lever has never been pulled."

Aidan stared at it silently, wondering.

"Then let us waste no time," Anvin said.

One at a time, all the men rushed forward. Dozens of men pressed close as they each grabbed hold of the massive stone lever, thirty feet long, and began to pull it down with all their might.

They groaned from the effort and Aidan watched, hopeful. Yet his heart fell as they finally stopped, all backing away, unable to budge it.

Leifall shook his head.

"As I feared," he said.

Aidan frowned.

"Is there no way to unlock it?" he demanded, impatient for his father's sake.

Leifall walked over to a small passageway, low to the ground, cut into the stone by a small arch. He got on his hands and knees and tried without success to squeeze through. Then he stood, red-faced, and shook his head.

"At the end of the passageway," he said, "there is a second lever. It might unlock the first. But we will never reach it. It was built to be hidden, inaccessible."

Aidan felt a rush of adrenaline, as he suddenly knew what he needed to do.

"I can fit!" he called out.

160

The men all turned to him in wonder. Aidan rushed forward, fell to his hands and knees, and examined the small stone passageway.

"I can fit!" Aidan insisted. "I can reach the second lever."

Anvin shook his head, grim.

"If you get stuck," Anvin said, "you will die. None of us can reach you."

"If I don't go," Aidan countered, "my father will die. What choice do I have?"

Without another word, Aidan turned and, heart pounding, began to squeeze himself into the tight, stone passageway.

It was airless in here, the stone pressing in from all directions, and Aidan had never felt more scared. He was barely able to move, and the farther in he crawled, the harder it was to breathe. He was soon forced to crawl on his stomach, on his elbows, and he felt huge, sticky spiders crawling on his face. He was breathing rapidly, yet he was unable to free his hands to swat them away.

Aidan crawled farther and farther, his elbows and forearms scraped up, feeling as if this would never end.

And then, suddenly, to his horror, he was trapped. Stuck.

Wiggling as he did, Aidan could not break fee.

He broke out in a sweat as panic set in.

Aidan had a flash that this was the pivotal moment of his short life. He finally understood what it meant to be a warrior, to be a man. It meant to be alone. To be utterly alone. And to rely on no one but yourself for your survival.

Aidan knew he had to find the courage, the strength, to do this. For himself. For his father. For his people. He thought of how much his father had struggled, what he had overcome, and he knew that he, too, could find the strength somewhere within himself. He knew he could summon some part of himself that was stronger than he thought. He *had* to.

He did not want to die in here.

Come on, Aidan willed himself.

Aidan dug in with his elbows ever harder, bleeding, ignoring the pain, and shoved his face in the dirt, using his toes. He groaned and groaned, feeling as if he were being crushed in a vise, until finally, in one great burst, he managed to move again. At first he moved an inch, then more, then a foot. He squeezed and pushed, farther and farther.

Suddenly he heard a noise behind him, a bark. He glanced back and was elated to see White racing into the cave. He rushed in, all the way, able to fit, until he finally reached Aidan. From behind, he lowered his head into Aidan's body and nudged him with all his might. Aidan was shocked at the wild dog's strength and determination to save him.

Moments later, Aidan finally burst through to a clearing, to his own shock and joy coming out on the other side. He emerged into sunlight, so relieved, and hugged White as the dog licked him back.

Coughing up dust, Aidan managed to stand upright, finding himself in a small chamber within the cave. The roar of the water was deafening in here. He was covered in spray, but the icy waters felt good, washing all the dust off his face and hair. It felt good to be alive.

Aidan wiped water from his eyes, caught his breath, and took stock. He looked around, examining the place, until finally he spotted it.

The stone lever.

This one was much smaller than the other, and he ran over to it, jumped up on it, grabbed with both hands, and yanked down.

Yet, to his dismay, nothing happened.

He tried again, planting his feet against the wall and pulling.

Yet still nothing.

Refusing to give up, Aidan jumped atop the lever and pulled again and again, groaning and crying, his hands cut from the stone. He yanked and yanked with all that he had, all that he was.

Come on, he willed, sweat stinging his eyes.

And then finally, to his own shock, it happened. To his delight, he felt the lever move beneath his hand, heard the sound of stone scraping stone. It moved slowly, his arms shaking, lower and lower—until finally, in one great motion, it hit the bottom.

There came a great cheer on the other side of the tunnel, and as Aidan got back down in the passage and squeezed his way back, easier this time as he was slick with water, he emerged on the far side just in time to see all the men, with one great cheer, pushing the great lever all the way down. He had unlocked it after all.

Aidan followed as the other men ran excitedly to the outer ledge of the cave. There came a great rumble from somewhere high above, slowly building, and as they all stood there and watched, looking out over the desert landscape far below, suddenly Aidan saw a sight he would never forget.

A river of water came gushing down the side of the cliff in what sounded like a massive explosion. It was as if an entire ocean were falling down before them.

Aidan watched as the falls actually changed course, as mountains of water gushed down the other side, rushed across the desert, and ambled their way somewhere for the horizon—and somewhere, he prayed, for the canyon.

Somewhere, for his father.

CHAPTER THIRTY FOUR

Duncan scrambled his way up the canyon wall, the ascent so steep he was nearly vertical, clawing his way up the canyon face. Dry rock and dirt gave way and Duncan slipped again and again before regaining his footing, as did his men around him, hundreds of men in their armor clanging their way up to freedom.

It was a desperate scramble. Duncan tried to control his panic as he looked back over his shoulder and saw the tens of thousands of Pandesians closing in, pursuing them across the canyon floor and now beginning to ascend the canyon face behind them. Worse, many of them stopped, lined up, and began to fire arrows.

Duncan braced himself as there came the ping all around him of metal arrowheads hitting stone, chipping away at small pieces of rock. Cries and shrieks rang out and he looked over and was pained to see too many of his men with arrows piercing their backs. As he watched, they lost their grip and fell backwards to their deaths.

Duncan reached out and grabbed for his friend, one of his oldest, most trusted soldiers, just feet away from him, who had an arrow plunged into his back. His eyes opened wide as he began to fall, and as Duncan swiped for him, he felt an awful pit in his stomach as he just missed him, unable to reach him in time.

"No!" Duncan shrieked.

Watching him die enraged Duncan. It made him want to turn around and charge the Pandesians below.

Yet he knew that would be shortsighted. He knew the key to victory lay just twenty feet above, at the very top of the canyon ridge. He knew what his men needed most was not to stand and fight, but to get out of there before the great flood came. *If* it ever came.

"CLIMB!" Duncan boomed to his men, trying to encourage them.

As he climbed, arrows and spears hitting the wall all around him, Duncan flinched, realizing how close they were coming. He realized what a vulnerable position he had put his men in, how reckless and desperate this whole strategy was. If for some reason Leifall did not come through, was unable to divert the waters of Everfall, the Pandesians would catch up to them as soon as they surfaced and slaughter him and all his men for good. Yet if the waters did come before Duncan's men could ascend and get out of their way, then he and his men would be drowned, washed away by the tidal wave, killed together with all the Pandesians below.

The chances of this mission succeeding were dire; yet the alternative, facing a much greater army in the open field, was not great, either.

Duncan's heart slammed as he looked up and saw the edge of the canyon looming. He groaned as he took his last step on a ledge and threw himself to the desert floor.

He lay there, gasping, and immediately spun around, reached down and grabbed as many of his men's hands as he could, yanking them up out of the canyon, dodging arrows as they sailed by. Every muscle in his body ached and burned, yet he would not stop until his men were all safe.

As the last of his men reached the desert floor, Duncan immediately stood and checked the horizon, hopeful.

Yet his heart fell. There came no river, no flood. And that could only mean one thing: Leptus had failed.

Yet Duncan knew that he could not give up hope, and that if the surging waters did come, there would be no time to lose. He turned to his men.

"PART WAYS!" he commanded.

He sprinted, and his men ran, too, forking, dividing their forces, half led by him and half by one of his commanders. Parting ways would also make it harder for the Pandesians to hunt them down.

Duncan sprinted, even though no water was in sight, hoping and praying. With every step, he also at least distanced himself from the Pandesians. Although, looking out ahead to the wasteland, Duncan knew there was nowhere left to run.

Duncan checked back over his shoulder, and his heart dropped to see the first Pandesian surface from the canyon. Behind him followed another.

Then another.

Hundreds of them followed, crawling over the edge like ants, out of the canyon, soon on their feet and rushing his way.

Duncan knew, in that moment, that all was lost. His plan had failed.

And then it came.

It began as a rumble, sounding like distant thunder. Duncan looked up before him, and he was breathless.

It appeared an entire ocean was gushing right for him, rumbling, its waves rolling, huge and white across the dry, dusty plains. It moved faster than anything he had ever seen, more powerful, more violent.

The Pandesians behind him were clearly shocked, too. They stopped in their tracks, gaping, as the waters raced right for them. Duncan and his men had parted ways, had made room for the river. But the Pandesians, having just emerged, still stood right in its path.

All the Pandesians scrambled to turn back around, to get out of the way of the water, stampeding each other. It was chaos as a logjam ensued, all of them trapped, all staring death in the face.

Duncan stood there and watched as the roaring waters gushed by him and then, a moment later, crashed down, smashing all the Pandesians like ants.

The waters continued, raging down into the canyon, landing at its bottom with a tremendous crash and spray, and filling it foot by foot. Duncan heard, just for a moment, the horrible shrieks from tens of thousands of soldiers still in the canyon, all crushed by the waters.

Soon, though, the shrieking stopped. The water stopped. The canyon was filled. Pandesian corpses floated over its edge, onto the dirt.

And finally, all was still.

Duncan stood there, and he and all his men slowly turned to each other and looked at each other in shock. And then, as one, they let out a great shout of victory.

Finally, they had won.

CHAPTER THIRTY FIVE

Ra walked slowly through the barren wasteland, alone, far from his army. In the distance, he could hear their shouts and cries, and he watched with indignation as the great waterfalls of Everfall poured down in a river, flooded the canyon. Down below, deep in the canyon, tens of thousands of his men were dying, drowning. Duncan had outsmarted him once again.

Ra burned with fury. Ra, of course, had other armies elsewhere in Escalon, but these were the vanguard of his men, the elite, and watching them all die in that trap of a canyon burned him to no end. Not because he cared about them—he did not—but because it would hamper his own cause, his own mission to wipe out Escalon for good. Hearing them die, Ra was all the more grateful he had not joined them this time. Instead, he had let his generals lead the battle and had furtively separated himself, marching through the desert alone, embarking on his backup plan. Duncan had won the battle—but Ra would win the war. Duncan was smart—but Ra was smarter.

Now, as Ra marched, with each and every step he mulled over his plan. Walking alone through the desert, he aimed for the far side of the canyon, where he could already see Duncan's men emerging, all of them alive, cheering, triumphant at their victory. They thought they had won, that they had vanquished the Holy and Supreme Ra. And in one sense they had.

Yet they were about to learn why Holy and Supreme Ra had never been vanquished. As he walked toward Duncan now, Duncan would give him a very different reception. Duncan would not meet him with a sword and shield, but an embrace, a hug.

For his appearance as he walked this desert was not that of a soldier, not that of the Holy and Supreme Ra —but rather, that of a girl. To the outside world, to even the most trained eye—even her father—he would appear not as the Great Ra.

But as Kyra.

He bore her features, her face, her body, her dress. Khtha had done his work well.

Ra would get close, so close that, in a father's embrace, he would finally have his chance to kill Duncan once for all.

He did not need his army. Just himself. And a bit of sorcery. Deception, after all, always triumphed over might.

Ra grinned wide.

Wait for me, Father, he thought. *Your daughter is coming.*

CHAPTER THIRTY SIX

Kyra walked slowly between the soaring pillars, the blackened stone rising to the heavens, and stopped at the threshold of this dead and ancient city of Marda. As she walked, she passed dozens of heads of trolls, of humans, impaled on pikes, to welcome her. It was clearly a sign to beware—yet this city hardly needed any more signs. It was the most ominous place she had ever laid eyes upon. Its buildings looked as if they had been forged from the stones of hell, black as night. A cold, damp draft blew through the empty, rubble-strewn streets, giving her a chill. Somewhere a creature wailed, and she could not tell if it were up ahead, or in the wind. She felt as if she'd entered a city of the dead.

Kyra trod slowly down the broad, main boulevard, feeling this place was abandoned. The dead silence was punctuated only by the occasional calling of a crow, perched high up somewhere, staring down as if mocking her, as if goading her on to her death. Black stone, black doors, windowless buildings lined streets paved in black granite, all of it framed by towering mountains of black. She looked down and saw that, carved into the stone, were five-pointed stars etched in scarlet red. Were they carved of blood? What did they symbolize?

Kyra felt the true presence of evil here, and the deeper she went, the more it clung to her. She had felt safer even in the thicket of thorns, confronting that monster, than she did here in this wide-open city of hell, with all these vacant buildings, all the heads everywhere, dripping blood as if just killed. She felt at every turn as if something were watching her, waiting to pounce. She gripped her staff tight, her knuckles white. What she wouldn't give to have Andor and Leo by her side now. Not to mention Theon.

Yet Kyra forced herself to be brave, to continue on. She could sense the Staff of Truth lay somewhere up ahead, sense that she had, at last, reached her final destination. She felt it burning in her veins, a sixth sense telling her how close she was, and with every step, it grew stronger. It was like her destiny calling.

Kyra walked cautiously, her staff clicking in the rubble, turning down narrow streets, beneath small stone archways, until finally the city opened in a wide, square plaza. In the center sat a statue of a massive stone gargoyle, scowling down, its mouth a fountain, vomiting lava into a pool as if it were blood. Kyra walked past it and was horrified to see it was real blood, splashing everywhere.

Kyra continued on through the streets, until finally the mountains beyond it loomed larger and she realized she was reaching the end of the city. She saw in the distance a massive stone wall ringing the city, its stones plastered with blood. At the city's end she spotted a huge arch, an exit gate, leaving the city. A portcullis hovered at its top, its sharpened spikes pointed down, as if waiting to sever the head of whoever passed beneath them, all dripping with blood.

Kyra felt a drop on her shoulder, then another. She held out a palm and examined it. It was red.

She looked up to the sky as more drops fell, and she was shocked to see that it was raining blood.

Kyra walked to the gate, stopped, and examined it. Its opening, she was horrified to see, was stretched with the biggest spider web she had ever seen, fifty feet high and just as wide. It was so massive and thick, at first she thought it was a rope. She stared, horrified, and did not want to ponder what sort of spider had spun it.

Kyra looked past the web, and as she did, her heart stopped. There, on the far side of it, stood a black, granite pedestal rising from the earth. And atop it sat a shining, black staff. Kyra was breathless. The Staff of Truth. She could sense it even from here.

It shone, a beacon in the gloom, lighting up the twilight, sticking straight up to the sky, as if inviting someone to grab it.

Kyra stepped toward the web, tentatively, sensing a trap. She sensed this was her final test—and perhaps her most intense one of all.

Kyra inched closer to the web, breathing hard, and raised her staff. She held it out before her, heart pounding in her throat as she reached out and touched the tip of it to the web. The web was thicker and stickier than she thought, and her staff stuck to it. She pulled back with all her might, and the entire web shook. To her shock, it was so sticky, she could not extract her staff.

Suddenly, without warning, the web recoiled, and Kyra felt herself being pulled, like a spring. A second later she was flying up in the air, and into the web.

170

Kyra was stunned as she felt herself weightless, and found herself stuck to the web, her back up against it, her arms spread out at her sides like a trapped insect. She writhed, panicked, yet was unable to move. She tried with all her might, yet she could not break free. Her staff lay in the web, too, stuck, several feet away from her, just out of reach.

Panic welled up inside her. She could not fathom how it had all happened so quickly. And the more she struggled, the more entangled she became.

Kyra slowly turned, her hair standing on end, as she heard an awful crawling noise. She looked up, and out of the corner of her eye, she was filled with dread to spot a creature that made her heart stop. There, crawling for her, sharing the same web, was the biggest spider she had ever seen—ten feet wide, with enormous, fuzzy black claws, massive red fangs, and beady red eyes.

Kyra's eyes widened in terror as it inched toward her, one grotesque claw at a time. She looked around, desperate, and suddenly saw all the bones in the web. She realized hundreds of sojourners had died here, people, like her, who had thought they could retrieve the Staff.

The spider crawled faster, bearing down on her, and Kyra, trapped, knew with a sudden horror that she would die here, in this awful place, by the fangs of this creature, on the edge of hell, where no one would even hear her scream.

With its strong atmosphere and complex characters, NIGHT OF THE BOLD is a sweeping saga of knights and warriors, of kings and lords, of honor and valor, of magic, destiny, monsters and dragons. It is a story of love and broken hearts, of deception, ambition and betrayal. It is fantasy at its finest, inviting us into a world that will live with us forever, one that will appeal to all ages and genders.

"If you thought that there was no reason left for living after the end of the Sorcerer's Ring series, you were wrong. Morgan Rice has come up with what promises to be another brilliant series, immersing us in a fantasy of trolls and dragons, of valor, honor, courage, magic and faith in your destiny. Morgan has managed again to produce a strong set of characters that make us cheer for them on every page....Recommended for the permanent library of all readers that love a well-written fantasy."
--Books and Movie Reviews, Roberto Mattos (regarding Rise of the Dragons)

About Morgan Rice

Morgan Rice is the #1 bestselling and USA Today bestselling author of the epic fantasy series THE SORCERER'S RING, comprising seventeen books; of the #1 bestselling series THE VAMPIRE JOURNALS, comprising eleven books (and counting); of the #1 bestselling series THE SURVIVAL TRILOGY, a post-apocalyptic thriller comprising two books (and counting); and of the new epic fantasy series KINGS AND SORCERERS. Morgan's books are available in audio and print editions, and translations are available in over 25 languages.

Morgan loves to hear from you, so please feel free to visit www.morganricebooks.com to join the email list, receive a free book, receive free giveaways, download the free app, get the latest exclusive news, connect on Facebook and Twitter, and stay in touch!

Lightning Source UK Ltd.
Milton Keynes UK
UKOW06f1325050216

267818UK00001B/8/P